DARE TO CONQUER

BARBARA RAE ROBINSON

Contact at barbararae@gmail.com

Cover design by Christy Keerins

Dare to Conquer / Barbara Rae Robinson

First edition

EBOOK ISBN: 978-0-9971824-4-6

PRINT ISBN: 978-0-9971824-5-3

❀ Created with Vellum

This book is dedicated to Maggie Lynch, friend and mentor. And also to the #ftb group and the goal reporting group whose members encouraged me and supported me for a long time. I couldn't have done this without your help.

CHAPTER 1

A taxi slowed, then stopped in front of his house. Doug Landreth set down his coffee cup. His Saturday morning had changed from warm and lazy to intriguing. He limped to the screen door.

A young woman got out. She saw him behind the screen, but stayed by the taxi with a suitcase and backpack. "I think you're my dad." Her voice was tentative, almost child-like, though she was definitely not a child.

He sucked in a breath. Could it be? But which daughter? "What's your name?"

"I'm Dani. My real birth certificate says Dani Landreth."

Tears welled up. "I'm your dad." He unlocked the screen door and opened it.

She waved off the taxi.

He couldn't take his eyes off of Dani. "It's been eighteen years since your mother disappeared with you girls. She told me being married to me was too dangerous."

"I wanted to come sooner."

She moved closer, up the short walkway. His heart constricted, making breathing near impossible. Her eyes, the gold flecks in the brown. Jenny's eyes. Jenny's brown hair, though a bit longer. Jenny's beautiful flawless skin.

"Why come now?"

"My sister's dead. Lindi's dead." She choked out the words.

Doug's heart shattered. The last time he'd held Lindi, she was barely a year old.

"What happened?" He pulled Dani into the house. Took the suitcase and backpack and dropped them to the floor. Pulled her into his arms and held her tight. "Who killed her?"

She nestled into his arms like she did as a four-year-old. "That gang guy who ran us out of Los Angeles when Lindi and I were little. A drive-by shooting." Her words were muffled by his shirt.

"How do you know it was Ramon Moreno?"

She leaned back and looked up at him. "Mom got a note, signed Moreno. Said I was next."

"No. No you won't be next." Bone deep anger leeched through his words. "I'll make sure he doesn't get you too."

He limped to the couch and she sat down beside him. "Where did your mother take you when you left Los Angeles?"

"Nebraska, where her grandparents were, then Florida, after they died. That's when she changed our names and got us fake birth certificates. She said she had to hide us, keep us away from you. For our safety."

A blaze of anger soared through him. "It didn't work."

"Why did that man kill Lindi?" A tear slipped down her cheek.

"Moreno wants revenge. Five years ago I killed his two younger sons during a drug raid. They were shooting at us. I took two lives to save three."

She pulled back, her eyes moist. "So I was lucky I was away from home. I had a job for the summer near my college. Mom said I had to leave and come here. That you'd protect me. Said that's what you do, like protect people." Her words held a hopeful note.

"That's part of what I do. But he's going to come here after me too. He wants me dead."

"So I'm not safe here either?" Her brows knit together and her face turned ashen.

"I'm sorry. No, not completely. Ramon Moreno plans to come to Portland. To take over the drug trade in the northwest."

"Oh."

"And kill me. He intends to finish the job he tried to do in Los Angeles."

"You're like crippled?" She sat up straight and looked down at his legs.

"A car bomb killed my second wife and shattered my legs. I'm lucky I still have both of them."

"Moreno did that?"

"He sent the guys who planted the bomb. So, yes, he did it."

"What do I do now? Do I run someplace else, far away?" Her voice held a note of panic.

"No. But you may have to hide in a safe place around here until we get rid of Moreno. There's a federal task force after him. He's a big drug trafficker now."

"Okay. I'll do what you say." She glanced at his cup on the end table. "Do you have more coffee? I'm awful tired. I took a red-eye from Miami."

"Sure I have coffee. Did you have breakfast?"

"No. And I'm hungry. I came straight from the airport. Do you have any cereal?"

Pride welled inside him. Dani seemed level-headed and

wasn't falling apart. He had one daughter back. His mood darkened. Because Lindi was dead.

Moreno had to be stopped. Before he killed Dani too.

Dani followed him to the kitchen and he pulled out cereal and milk and set them on the breakfast bar. He poured her a cup of coffee and refreshed his own. Then sat beside her and picked up his cup.

The phone rang. He grabbed the receiver from the charger. Caller ID blocked. He glanced at Dani.

And answered the call.

"One down, one to go." The voice was unmistakable. Doug's grip tightened, nearly smashing the phone into pieces. "Pretty little thing, isn't she? So was the one who died."

Doug seethed inside. "Moreno...you are scum." He kept his language in check. What he wanted to say, he wouldn't say in front of Dani.

She put her spoon down and hunched over, seeming to draw inside herself.

"Soon all those around you will be dead." Moreno cackled, like he'd made a big joke. "Then you and me, we have a show down. And I win."

Except Moreno didn't joke. He was deadly serious when it came to revenge. And killing for sport.

"Killing young girls is shit-ass cowardice." This time he said it out loud.

"You killed two of my sons. I kill your two daughters. I know where the other one is. In your house."

A chill cascaded through Doug despite the warmth of the July morning. "Where are you?"

"I'm here." The phone went dead.

DOUG SET down his cell phone and shifted on the couch, stretching out his aching right leg. Four calls made. Business at Landreth Investigations would not be normal for a while.

Chet would let the rest of the police department know what happened. Doug's very efficient office manager, Meagan, would notify the staff of an emergency meeting and tell Alison to come to his house first. Nick would protect Tricia, since she's family. And Dave would hide Dani in his house for now.

Two more calls to make.

The shower turned off down the hall. Dani would be out soon.

Could he protect her? At times he felt weak, helpless, disabled. Yet he still had his upper body strength. And his intelligence. He'd outwit Moreno. Outwit his hired guns. Outwit those who wrote him off as a helpless cripple.

He picked up the phone and called Scott. "Now, like immediately. Lindi is dead. Dani is here. Moreno is in town. Get as much up as you can by ten, for an agency meeting."

"Oh, shit. I'm on it." The line went dead.

Doug refilled his coffee cup, then returned to the couch to tackle the hardest call. How could he convince his very stubborn mother she had to leave town for a while? She answered on the second ring.

"Are you going to come see me today?" She used her you-don't-spend-enough-time-with-me tone.

"No." A twinge of guilt tightened his gut. A word he rarely used with her. "We've got problems. I want you to take a vacation. Leave now, today if possible, and stay away until I tell you it's safe to come back." He waited for her outburst.

"I will not." Right on cue. "I won't go away because someone doesn't like you."

The cramp in his right leg worsened, but he tried to ignore

the pain. "It's more complicated than that." He kept his tone level, matter-of-fact, and explained what happened. "I don't want anything to happen to you."

"That drug guy isn't my problem."

"Mom." This time he let his exasperation show in his voice. "I'm afraid Moreno will go after you, since you're family. He said he's going to kill Dani."

"I want to see my granddaughter. And I'm hosting a luncheon here in three days. I can't pack a suitcase and leave town."

"But that's exactly what you need to do. Now." He infused his tone with all his frustration. "You could go up to my place in the woods for a few days."

"That's too far. I won't leave my house."

Dani appeared in the doorway to the living room, wearing jeans and a T-shirt, looking like the college student she was.

"I'll talk to you again later. I have to go." He ended the call. Somehow he had to convince her to leave.

"I have a grandma here in Portland?"

"Yes, she lives here and she's as stubborn as she ever was."

"Will Moreno hurt her too?"

"I hope not, but we can't count on it. I'll think of something."

A car pulled into the driveway, then Alison Steele appeared on the porch. He unlocked the screen door and let her in. "Thanks for coming."

"I'm so sorry." She reached out and touched his arm. The warmth quickly became an ache throughout his body. The first time she'd ever touched him on purpose.

She pushed her chin-length blond hair away from her face. "And this must be Dani."

He introduced them.

"Alison, take Dani to Dave's house. He knows she's coming.

He got home last night from his month in Tennessee, finding those runaways. I'm counting on Moreno's men not knowing about him yet."

"Why would Moreno come after her here?"

"Moreno is in town and has someone watching the house. He knows Dani is here. Look for a tail when you leave."

"Will do." She looked directly at him, her soft blue eyes meeting his. "You take care too." Something flickered between them, a connection of sorts.

The timing was off. He lowered his gaze. "He's planning to kill those around me before he gets to me. I'm safer than she is. Or even you."

Alarm flashed on Alison's face. She got it.

"I told Meagan to take her family and go on vacation, but first to rent another apartment in the building where you live, in case we need it."

"This is really serious."

"Yes. One more thing before you leave. Dani needs a cell phone that can't be traced." He limped over to a cabinet and brought out a cell phone and handed it to Dani. "This is a phone that has my number and all the agency people programmed into it. We all use these phones to communicate when there's a problem. Don't use anything but this one." He stared into her eyes "And don't call your mother."

"Oh. Okay. When will I see you again?" Dani's words were plaintive.

"I don't know. I'll figure something out so we can be together. But not tonight." He tried to keep the frustration out of his voice. Dani might misinterpret it. He wanted her with him, but knew she'd have a better chance surviving with other members of his team.

"Let's go, Dani." Alison's eyes met his again. "I'll make sure she's safe with Dave."

"Then come to the office for the meeting at ten."

Dani went back to the bedroom and reemerged with her suitcase and backpack.

Doug gave her a hug, not wanting to let her go. But he had to. "Stay safe. I have very competent people working for me. They'll protect you."

Stark fear flared in her eyes.

CHAPTER 2

*A*lison backed out of Doug's driveway. Her Taurus was the only vehicle on the winding, tree-lined road. But a tail could be waiting at the bottom of the hill.

A stab of guilt pierced her. She hadn't thought about someone following her from her apartment to Doug's house. Underestimating Moreno could get them killed.

"I don't want my dad to die." Dani's words were soft but forceful. "I don't want to lose him now. I've just found him."

Alison's heart clenched, like it was wrapped in tight bands. "I know. I don't want anything to happen to him either." That something that passed between them in his living room had sparked a fierce desire inside her. She would do everything she could to protect him. And not because he was her boss.

She turned onto a street lined with older, stately houses and wound around several blocks, watching for a tail. An Hispanic man in an old beater kept pace with them, a half block behind.

"Do you have that cell phone handy that your dad gave you?"

"Yeah."

"Find your dad's number and call him. Tell him to call Chet and have a patrol car pick off that car behind us." She gave Dani the description of the old brown Pontiac and their location. They weren't close enough for her to read the license plate.

Dani made the call.

Alison continued circling the same three blocks until the patrol car arrived and stopped the Pontiac. She gave a honk of recognition and sped off, straight for Burnside. "That took care of that guy."

"What would have happened if the police hadn't come?" Panic rode Dani's voice.

"I would have had to lose him some other way. This was easier. I was hoping the police were ready to help us." Time to change the subject. "So, you didn't know where your father was?"

"No. Mom wouldn't tell us. Said it was too dangerous for us to know. But Lindi got killed anyway."

Alison headed for the Burnside Bridge. Dave's place was at least four miles from Doug's house. She planned on a few extra turns on the other side of the river to make sure she wasn't picked up by another tail.

"Moreno must have planned his revenge for years. He spent four years down in Mexico before heading back to Los Angeles to rebuild his drug empire there."

"Can't they just like arrest him?"

"They have to find him first. He's intelligent and knows what he wants. Mainly lots of money. And revenge against your father."

"Was my dad trying to arrest his sons?"

"Yes. They were drug dealers and your dad was with other officers trying to arrest six gang members. The sons were the ones out front shooting so they got killed. Your dad happened to fire the shots that took them down."

"Dumb luck." Dani pointed to her right. "Hey, what's that river we're crossing over?"

"The Willamette. It cuts Portland into two parts, west side and east side."

"Pretty river. Was my dad a good policeman?"

Alison relaxed a bit as the conversation shifted. Dani didn't miss much, but flitted from thought to thought. "I've heard your father was an excellent policeman, then an excellent detective. Now he runs a highly respected private investigation agency."

"Mom never said any of that. Just called him a hot head cop."

"From what I've heard, he was never that." Alison was sure of it. She'd seen him in action in Portland.

"Did I do the right thing, coming here?" Dani blurted it out.

Alison hesitated, choosing her words carefully. Dani might be twenty-two, but she was still young and inexperienced. "Yes, I think you did the right thing. Your best chance is with your dad. With us. But you have to understand there may be a shoot-out with Moreno before this is over. It could happen fast."

"So I'm still in danger." It was a statement, not a question.

"Yes. We all are. But you'll be surrounded by people who can protect you. Back there in Florida, all by yourself, you would have been killed by now."

Dani blew out a breath. "I thought so. And Mom did too. That's why I'm here."

Alison turned off Burnside and drove around a few more blocks. No one followed them. She drove another mile down a tree-lined street and stopped in front of a small white house. "Dave Quinlan lives here. He's been out of town. Your dad is hoping Moreno doesn't have him flagged as an agency employee yet. You'll stay with him today, and I'll be back later."

"You're going to go to that meeting?"

"Yes, I have to be there. I imagine I'll be coordinating your protection and spending my nights wherever you are."

"So I won't see much of my dad for a while." Another statement.

"I'm afraid so." She hesitated again. Wondering how much to tell Dani. "Let's go inside, and I'll explain to both of you what's going on."

Dave had the door open by the time they got out of the car. He looked every bit the biker he was. T-shirt that hugged his biceps. Tattoos on his arms. Chain with a clunky metal pendant around his neck. He fit in places where other agency members couldn't. Alison glanced at Dani. Her wide-eyed stare said it all. She was not impressed.

Alison would have to get back as soon as she could.

ALISON CARRIED DANI'S BACKPACK, and Dani wheeled her suitcase up to the porch. Dave stepped down and picked up the suitcase, giving Dani the once-over. His gaze registered approval. Dani cringed and backed up.

"Dave, this is Doug's daughter, Dani. She's here for your protection." She stared at him until he looked away sheepishly.

"Glad to meet you, Dani." His tone was formal and the wolfish leer gone.

He led them into the living room, and Dani and Alison sat on the couch. Dani's eyes lit up at the sight of the big screen TV. Something to keep her occupied. Good.

Dave slouched in a facing chair. "I got Doug's quick version of what happened. You going to explain, Alison?"

She recapped for him the events of the morning, including

the killing of Lindi. "So our goal is to keep Dani hidden and hope Moreno's gang can't find her."

"And I've been out of town, so my house is the logical first choice. Good thinking on Doug's part." A measured tone and none of the profanity he often used.

Alison scooted closer to Dani and patted her on the arm. "Since we know Moreno is now in the area, we have to be doubly careful. And watch for tails at all times."

"Have you dealt with one?" That quizzical left eyebrow of his shot up.

"A cop had to pick him off."

He laughed, his usual easy laugh that often broke any tension surrounding him.

Dani frowned, still focused on his biker dude persona.

"Doug mentioned a DEA agent joining the agency. What's up?" Back to seriousness.

"Doug's not sure, but the DEA offered him to the agency as liaison to the federal task force that's targeting Moreno. Jake Wilson will be introduced at the staff meeting you'll be missing. He'll coordinate between the federal task force and any police agencies involved."

Dave leaned forward. "It will end in a fire fight. I've always said that."

"You could be right. We have to be ready if and when it happens."

Dani twisted her hands in front of her. "I'm scared."

"We'll take care of you and not let him get to you." Dave's sincere words were addressed directly to Dani. Her eyes widened.

She jumped up. "Is there anywhere I can be safe? Now?"

"We don't know for sure." Alison stood and pulled Dani into her arms for a hug. And her heart went out to the younger woman. Dani was just finding out about the seamier side of life, where drug wealth ruled and law enforcement had to run fast to keep up.

Dani wiggled free and sat on the couch again. "I'll be okay." Her words were shaky and she still looked scared. "I know I'm safer here than in Florida." Her eyes misted. The loss of her sister weighed heavily on her.

Alison stayed standing and gazed at Dani, willing her to be calm. "I'll be back as soon as I can. I'll be with you tonight, wherever you are. Probably here." She kept her words gentle.

"That would work." Dave stood. "I have a futon and you two can have the bed in the bedroom at the back of the house."

"When I return, I'll bring food. You two stay inside. Keep the doors locked."

"Will do." Dave walked Alison to the door. "You're a target too, you know. We all are." He said it quietly. "Moreno knows you're the crack shot on the team."

"So we all stay vigilant and protect Dani and Doug and hope for the best." She attempted to keep her tone positive.

"Yeah." His green eyes darkened. "The alternative is death."

CHAPTER 3

*D*oug eased out of his chair and stood, extending his hand across his desk. "Welcome to the agency, Jake. Glad to have you with us. Let's go, so you can meet the others."

"I'm glad to be here." Jake Wilson's words were stiff. Like he wasn't sure of this assignment. He ran his hand through his short black hair, leaving spikes in the front.

Doug picked up his cane and limped around the desk. By the end of today Jake might be sorry he'd agreed to be in the middle of whatever Moreno had planned.

Jake stood and opened the office door and followed Doug into the hallway.

Kara Rasmussen's green eyes flashed. "Scott has the door locked."

"And my computer is missing." Erik Bergstrom raised his voice, something he rarely did.

Doug laughed. "All is well." He tapped on the conference room door with the cane. "Scott must want to show off his handy work to everyone at once."

The door opened and two men in overalls emerged, carrying tool boxes. They nodded at the waiting group and left by the side door.

"Come on in." Scott Armstrong gestured from the doorway.

Doug limped in. Jake followed him, then the other four filed in.

"Okay, new paneling. Why?" Alison's words were skeptical, demanding.

Doug nodded at Scott.

"This is our safe room. It's now the equivalent of a bullet-proof armored car." Scott's smug smile accompanied his words. "And no window in here to worry about."

Doug glanced around. It looked like any upscale boardroom, paneled in dark wood. But Scott had promised reinforced bulletproof walls.

Erik's computer had been moved to a desk in the corner, against the inner wall. He rushed in and over to his computer. As their technical guru and information expert, his computer was the most important in the agency.

The long oak conference table, with its ten chairs, dominated the middle of the room. A small refrigerator. A coffee pot. A counter for munchies. Doug smiled.

"Thank you, Scott. Good work." Doug sat at the head of the table. "This is our new command post. We'll work in here most of the time. Bring your desktop computers, laptops, files, whatever you need. Pile the table high if you want to."

"You're serious." Rafe Campbell pulled out a chair and sat.

"War time." Doug used his best commander in chief voice. "We're gearing up for whatever Moreno throws at us. And for however long it takes to bring him down."

He gazed at each one of them in turn. "I don't want any more deaths."

Jake stroked his short black beard and kept his green eyes averted. He'd question Jake further. Something bothered the man. He gestured to Jake to sit at his right. Everyone else took a seat.

"I'd like to introduce the newest member of our agency. Jake Wilson is officially DEA but assigned to our agency as liaison. He's a federal officer with full powers where drugs and dealers are concerned." He motioned to Jake to say something.

"I'm glad to be working with this agency." Jake's expression was sober. "The DEA is building a case against Moreno, so he can be tried in a court of law. Because of Moreno's interest in Doug, I'm here to keep tabs on everything he's doing, while we locate him and make plans to eventually arrest him." He frowned, a wrinkled brow kind of frown. "Seems this agency has entered the drug wars, prepared or not."

"So that's your assignment?" Erik sounded skeptical.

"For now. Our goal is everyone's safety while we go after Moreno. This may take a while."

Doug's gut clenched. Building a case. Arresting Moreno. Those words set off alarm bells in his body. Tightening the tension in his gut. Where would Jake's loyalty lie when the bullets started flying? And they would be flying. Moreno's agenda didn't jive with the DEA agenda. He didn't like Jake's use of the word eventually. Time was one commodity they didn't have.

Doug took a minute to introduce the agency investigators. When he got to Scott, Scott extended his hand to Jake, since he was sitting next to him. "I'm jack of all trades, including bullet proofer." Jake shook his hand.

"I should add that Erik is the computer whiz around here," Doug said. "Consult him for information."

"Glad to meet you all." Jake nodded several times.

Doug rapped for attention. "My daughter, Dani, is at Dave's house. Alison will be there tonight. We have to keep Moreno from killing Dani, or anyone else. I'm more worried about all of you than myself. I'm last on his list."

He hesitated, then took a deep breath. "Moreno's exact words to me this morning were, 'Soon all those around you will be dead. Then you and me, we have a show down. And I win.'"

"Wow." Alison scrutinized the paneling. "Scott's handiwork may save our lives."

Doug shifted in his chair, stretching out his bum leg. "But this room only works during the day. I'm worried about the rest of the time."

Jake cleared his throat. "I've been authorized by the DEA to set up a safe house for all of us, if it's needed."

Doug stared at him. "It's needed. What are they willing to do for us?"

"Rent a big house in an area that's easy to get in and out of. The local police will provide protection."

"How soon?"

Jake lifted his chin. "I'll go see a realtor when I leave here." He grinned. "I'm only too happy to do it. I spend too much time in motels."

Kara stood and grabbed the coffee pot on the sideboard. She started around the table, refreshing everyone's coffee. "So anyone who wants strength in numbers can move in there temporarily?"

"That's the idea," Jake said. "I didn't realize that everyone in this agency is in danger. That was news to me."

"Are you sorry you're with us?" Doug had to ask.

"No. Danger comes with my job." Jake picked up his coffee cup. His expression was once again somber.

As were all the other faces in the room. Doug's gut clenched.

He hated that his job down in Los Angeles had now endangered these people he worked with and cared about here in Portland. "Any questions so far?" His gaze lingered on Alison.

"Yes," Rafe said. "You knew this guy down in L.A. What was his favorite way of taking someone out? What should we be watching for?"

"Very good question." Doug shifted in his chair. "When it was an individual, usually a lone gunman did a drive-by shooting or an execution in private. Sometimes strafing with automatic rifle fire. That's why the bulletproofing. He also burned out a few of his enemies."

"Molotov cocktails? Things like that?" Kara asked.

"Yes. I remember one instance when he fire-bombed the house of a relative of the guy he was targeting. As a warning. The relative died." He sobered and looked away.

"Are you thinking of your mother, Doug?" Alison's words were soft, full of caring.

"Unfortunately yes. She refused to leave town when I called her this morning."

"I'll go to her house and check her smoke alarms," Scott said. "And I'll see what we can do to make it easy for her to get out if something happens. Does she sleep upstairs? Maybe a rope ladder out a window."

"I'll go too and see if there's something I can do to get her ready for an emergency evacuation." Alison's gaze met his, her blue eyes full of compassion.

"Thank you. Both of you." Doug turned to Scott. "Yes, her bedroom is upstairs. It has a deck off the back. A rope ladder would work there." He gazed around the room, catching the eye momentarily of each person. "We all need to think of every precaution we can take."

"What about Tricia?" Kara's words were demanding.

"I warned Nick. I'm sure he's arranging protection for her until this is over. Their baby is due in about a month."

"Do you think Moreno will escalate fast?" Erik asked.

"Yes. Moreno's going to get frustrated, when he can't find Dani and isolate her. He may start with someone else." He let his gaze linger a few seconds on each person. "That's why we have to be prepared."

His gaze stopped at Alison. "You're on Moreno's list because you were in Los Angeles last October, when you were on vacation. He knows you were there. And he knows your ties to the area."

"Is that why Eddie Velasquez was killed back in November?" Alison's expression showed surprise.

"Yes. I'm sorry I didn't warn you away from going. We lost a good man, a good contact."

"I knew too many people on Moreno's turf." Her words were apologetic. "It's where I grew up."

"Our pasts can come back to haunt us at any time." Again, he gazed around the table. "Please. Do everything you can to stay safe. And still do your job."

Then he turned to Erik." Make sure the cloud backups are working for our computer system. And keep the office computers shut down when not in use, so someone without a password can't get in."

"Are you taking your laptop with you?" Erik asked.

"Yes, I'll keep it with me. It doesn't have any of the very sensitive documents on it, but I can still use it for internet access and basic file access. I can get to the cloud stuff if I need it."

"For additional backups, I'll put everything on portable hard drives too. And stash them in that big safety deposit box Meagan opened for sensitive storage."

"Good thinking, Erik." Another glance around the table. "I think that does it. If anyone else has ideas, please speak up. All our lives are on the line."

"What about everything else we're working on?" Rafe asked.

"We have three clients right now who are priorities," Doug said. "We're committed to time lines. And this agency has a reputation to uphold."

"Shiller goes on trial next week," Rafe said.

"He's number one on the priority list," Doug said. "His defense lawyer is counting on us to get him the information that will help Shiller."

"And I have the information I needed from his lawyer, so I can run with the investigation," Rafe said. "Maybe another ten to twelve hours of work."

"Sounds good. If you get slowed down and need help, holler."

"I will."

"The insurance fraud case, Kara? Are they still in a rush?"

"Yes, the insurance company wants to clear this up as soon as possible and get a judgment against the men who set that arson fire."

"How much more time do you figure?"

"Not more than a week or two."

"Alison, are you completely finished with that case you had last week?"

"Yes. All wrapped up and the client is happy."

"Good. Your job is stick with Dani."

"Sure."

"Scott?"

"I'm free to do what needs to be done to keep all of us safe. I just finished that identity theft case, with Erik's computer help."

"Good. And Erik, you're still working the GPS surveillance of that cheating husband, aren't you?"

"Racking up the data. The client wants as much proof as we can give her. Big money involved."

"You can keep going on that, as time permits, and the three priority ones. Anything else gets pushed back for now." This time his glance stopped for a few seconds on each person around the table. "Our number one objective is staying alive."

CHAPTER 4

"*T*hat's the house." Nervous pulses of energy bounced around inside Alison.

Scott stopped in front of the large gray house with white trim. "Nice digs."

Those pulses of energy increased their tempo. Perfectly manicured lawn and flower beds. A lovely home. The kind of place the widow of a judge would live. The kind of place a young Doug had lived. Definitely a lifestyle out of her reach. She swallowed that thought. "Doug will be completely devastated if anything happens to his mother."

"It's our job to help." Scott opened the back of his SUV. "March in with authority. Doug said he'd call ahead." Scott grabbed his two duffel bags of gear.

Alison grabbed the other bag, traipsed up the narrow steps to the porch, and rang the doorbell.

The door opened almost immediately. "Alison and Scott?" Clipped words. Was she nervous too?

"Yes, Mrs. Landreth. May we come in?"

"Certainly." She stepped back and they entered. Her darting brown eyes showed wariness, yet her chin lifted slightly. Words came to Alison that she didn't normally use. Matronly, formidable. She had long curly gray hair pulled back in a ponytail. She wore gray slacks, and an orange tunic that looked like it came from Nordstrom. Shoes with sensible heels. Would this elegant woman agree to climb down a rope ladder?

Doug's mother shut and locked the door. Then led them into the living room.

Alison suppressed a smile. How long did it take Doug to get her into the habit of keeping the doors locked?

Alison set down her bag and sat on the couch. Scott sat in a chair, setting his bags next to his feet.

Mrs. Landreth chose the other end of the couch and eyed the bags suspiciously. "I guess you're going to tell me what to do if there's trouble." Her words were as guarded as her expression.

"What did Doug say when he called?" Scott asked.

"That you were coming. That you would tell me...show me how to prepare for an attack by that thug."

"Did he tell you what the possibilities might be, Mrs. Landreth?" Alison kept her tone neutral.

"No. He said you'd explain." A note of anger in her words. "And call me Betty. Mrs. Landreth sounds too stuffy."

"Thank you, Betty." Maybe that was progress. Would she trust them?

"Okay." Scott scooted to the edge of the chair. "Moreno's gang sometimes uses automatic rifle fire. You need to stay away from the front of the house. From the windows."

Her eyes widened.

"Sometimes they do drive by shootings. Getting from your house out to your car in the driveway could be a problem."

She brushed a wisp of hair back from her face. "What else?" Her tone was demanding.

"They've also used fire. Burned people out of their homes."

"Do you really think they might try to burn me out?"

"A big possibility." Scott's words were forceful. "Moreno's gang has used Molotov cocktails in Los Angeles. They're looking for ways to intimidate and isolate Doug. Attacking you could be part of their plan."

"We don't know what he's going to do next." Alison said the words quietly. "We can't take any chances. He had Lindi killed, he's after Dani, and Doug is last on his list." She hesitated. "I'm on his hit list. And because you're family, you could be a target too."

"The safest thing for you to do is get on a plane today and leave the state." Scott challenged her with his words and his expression.

"I'm not leaving. I have things to do. I don't think it's that serious." Her words were clipped, forceful.

And Alison's spirits tumbled. "I hope you're right." Alison shifted on the couch so she was looking directly at Betty. "But we can't take any chances with your life."

"First question." Scott reached for one of his bags. "How many smoke alarms do you have and where are they located?"

"There's two. One in the downstairs hallway. And one upstairs, near my bedroom."

"I'm going to check yours and put in fresh batteries, then I'll install about six more." He opened the bag and showed her the boxes of smoke detectors.

"Why so many?"

"For an immediate alarm, if a fire starts anywhere in the house. Time is crucial for getting out alive." Scott's words had a warning tone. "You sleep upstairs, right?"

"Yes."

"We'll have to improvise a way for you to get out, using your deck at the back of the house."

"There's no stairs there." Alarm showed on her face.

Scott kicked the other bag. "I brought a rope ladder. You're going to learn how to climb down without hurting yourself."

"I can't do that." Her words were loud and angry.

"I'll show you how," Alison said. "It's easy, really."

"No. I won't do it."

"You will if your life depends on it." Alison kept her eyes on Betty. Studying her reaction. Was it fear or stubbornness? Hopefully stubbornness. That could be overcome easier than fear of heights.

Scott stood. "Let's go check that deck." He picked up his two bags. Alison picked up the other. They followed Betty upstairs and into her bedroom at the back of the house.

Betty unlocked the slider to the deck and they went out into the July heat. The sun was high in the sky, shining directly on them. The backyard was shaded by several trees, but they weren't close to the house.

"This will do." Scott set down his bags. "I'm going to bolt the rope ladder to the deck and loop it over the top of the rail. You'll have to swing over the top of the rail and put your feet on the rungs. Then you can go down slowly."

"Oh, no. No."

"Scott, set it up," Alison said. "I'll demonstrate."

Betty's eyes widened, but she didn't say anything else. Alison knew desperation first hand. You do what you have to do to stay alive. She only hoped Betty had enough of a fighting spirit.

"Let's go back inside while Scott sets up the ladder." Alison followed Betty into the bedroom. "I have some more things to discuss with you."

They sat in the two chairs at a small round table in one corner. Alison pulled a backpack out of the bag she'd carried upstairs.

"This is your grab and go bag. Before you go to bed every night, make sure everything you need is in this backpack. Make sure you have a pair of shoes next to the bed. And a jacket on the bed you can grab and put on."

"I'm glad I sleep in pajamas, and not a gown." Betty's tone was ironic. No anger. A little bit of progress.

Alison smiled. "Yes, that will help. You'll keep a change of clothes in the bag at all times. And extra shoes, in case you don't have time to put on the shoes. At night you'll put your wallet, keys, and cell phone in there. Whatever you can't live without."

"You are serious, aren't you? You think something bad is going to happen."

"It could. You need to be prepared for the worst. And Moreno's worst is burning people out of their homes. Or shooting them."

"And I'm being silly staying here."

"Yes."

Betty took a deep breath. "I'm not leaving. So what else do I need to do?"

"Do you have some special jewelry or keepsakes you don't want to lose?"

"My husband kept guns in the house. He had a fireproof gun safe installed in the basement. I can put some things in that. My important papers are in my safe deposit box at the bank."

"Good. You're prepared. Find what you want to put in the backpack and the safe, and I'll check with Scott and Doug."

Alison went outside to the deck.

"The ladder is ready. I'll start on the smoke detectors." Scott stood and picked up his tools.

Alison peered over the railing. The ladder hung all the way to the ground. "Looks good. I'll show her how to use it when she's finished gathering her stuff."

She pulled out her cell phone and called Doug. "We're getting it done. She seems to be cooperating, though we haven't tested the rope ladder yet."

"Have you eaten lunch?"

"No. We've been too busy to think about it."

"I'll pick up pizza and come by. I want to talk to her again and bring her an agency phone."

"See you in a jiff." She ended the call.

"The backpack is ready." Betty gestured toward the bed. "Will you help me carry some things to the basement?"

"Sure." She glanced at the pile of jewelry boxes and trinkets on the bed. "Let's use this bag the backpack was in. She loaded most of Betty's valuables into it. Betty picked up what didn't fit.

Then she looked straight at Alison. "I am not going down that ladder." Her rebellious tone defied argument.

DOUG GRIPPED his cane tighter and edged up the shallow steps to his mother's porch. Throbbing pain coursed down his right leg. He clutched two pizzas balanced on his left arm. And nearly tipped backward. Pushing himself forward into the door frame, he breathed deep breaths and balanced on his stronger leg.

He could ring the doorbell and have someone let him in. Or, he could use his key and conceal the amount of pain he was in. He opted for the latter.

He hung his cane on his arm and unlocked the door. Then, using his cane, he made it into the kitchen and slid the pizzas onto the counter. And collapsed onto a bar stool.

The pain in his leg continued to throb. He sat for a couple of minutes, taking deep breaths, waiting for the pain to ease. When it was more tolerable, he leaned on his cane and limped into the hallway. Voices wafted down the stairway.

He called up the stairs. "Pizza in the kitchen. Anyone hungry?"

"Coming." Alison called down.

He limped back into the kitchen and sat at the table by the window where there was enough room for the four of them.

Alison got there first and sat next to him. She reached out and put a hand on his arm. "She won't leave, and she says she won't go down the ladder, but otherwise she's getting prepared for a fire. Is there a security system of any kind?"

The heat from her hand scalded his forearm. He put his other hand on top of hers. To prolong the contact. "No, no security system, yet. That's coming next. She's stubborn. She'll stay whatever the risk."

Alison pulled her hand away. "I hope nothing happens to her. We're doing what we can. We can only hope it's enough."

His first impulse was to grab her hand back. But he resisted. "Thanks for helping her." Alison was such a compassionate person. She had no idea how much he cared for her. But he had nothing to offer a woman like her. A battle-scarred body and legs too weak to defend her in a fight. He knew she'd had a troubled past and hoped she'd confide in him sometime.

"It's the least I could do. We still have to try the ladder, though. And at least show her how it works."

"Hmm. I couldn't climb down. I'd have to rappel." He laughed at himself. He heard footsteps and voices. Alison stood. A void existed where she had touched him.

His mother came into the kitchen, followed by Scott.

"Smells good. I don't usually eat pizza. But today I will. I'm living dangerously already."

"Glad you recognize that." Doug let sarcasm ride his words.

"Hrmph." Betty grabbed four plates from the cupboard and opened the pizza boxes.

They made quick work of the pizza and the iced tea Betty served to go with it.

"Everything is ready, except the testing of the ladder." Scott set down his tea glass. "Tomorrow our security guy will put in a system that will sound an alarm if there's a break in."

Betty stood and picked up plates. "Any alarm has to be loud to wake me."

"It will be. And a silent alarm to the security company. They'll send help immediately."

"The kind of system I've been wanting you to get for a long time," Doug said. "Now you're getting it, whether you want it or not."

His mother frowned at him, but didn't protest. Another battle won. He nodded his thanks to Scott, who smiled. Their plot worked.

Alison stood and helped clear the table. Betty put the remaining pizza in the refrigerator.

Doug smiled inwardly. His mother had a weakness for pizza. She'd eat the leftovers for dinner tonight.

Scott pushed back from the table. "Let's go try out that ladder."

"I'll stay below and watch." Doug limped to the back door and outside to the back patio. The summer sun beat directly down on him where he stood. He had to stay on the edge of the patio to see any activity on the deck above. He leaned on his cane to get as much weight from his right leg as he could.

His mother emerged first from the bedroom. Alison and

Scott followed. Alison put on a backpack, threw her leg over the rail, and found a foothold on the ladder. Then she eased her weight onto the ladder, and brought her other leg over the railing. Long legs, encased in denim. Jeans that fit snugly and showed off her enticing curves. *Don't go there.*

He looked away, but couldn't erase the image from his mind. What would she look like with less clothes? Or naked? *Definitely don't go there.*

His mother peered over the railing as Alison easily descended the ladder. The urge to go to Alison tugged at him. He stayed at the edge of the patio. The uneven lawn was difficult to walk on even when his leg wasn't bothering him.

Alison climbed back up the ladder and onto the deck. She took off the backpack and extended it to his mother. His mother stepped back as if hesitating.

"No. I'm not going to try that ladder today. If I need to, I'll use it."

She stomped into the house.

CHAPTER 5

*D*oug rounded the last curve on the uphill route to his house. From a distance everything looked okay. But he couldn't shake the chill that overtook him. Too much had happened. Lindi was dead. Dani was here and scared. His mother refused to leave town or try out the rope ladder.

How could this day get any worse?

The unmarked police car behind him passed him, turned around, pulled into a wide spot on the narrow street. Doug parked in front of his garage.

His gut clenched. Spasms of pain radiated out. The screen door and the front door stood ajar.

He slapped the steering wheel with his hand. "Damn." The day got worse. Another message from Moreno.

He patted the holster under his light jacket. A habit. Then pulled out his cell phone and sent a text to the officer in the parked car, asking him to call for backup and alert Chet Richardson.

He stepped outside his SUV to wait. He leaned on the vehicle, holding his cane in his left hand, keeping his right hand free to grab his automatic.

In a few minutes two patrol cars pulled up, one right after the other. He knew the officers. Shawn Murray and Ted Farmington, both veterans on the force.

He greeted the two men. "Check out the inside and see if anyone is hiding. And document the damage. I had visitors."

Murray frowned at him. "You knew it would happen. Why didn't you upgrade your security system?"

"You've been talking to Chet."

"Yeah. He said you'd do it now. He's on his way."

"Good. I'll wait in my car while you two see what happened inside." He opened the car door and sat on the edge of the driver's seat, his leg stretched out. Pain radiated down his right leg. He clenched his teeth.

He didn't have long to wait for Chet. He'd known Chet for many years. The older man was already a detective when Doug joined the Portland Police Bureau as a rookie patrolman.

Chet stopped on the driveway near the car. "Ted and Shawn inside?"

"They're looking for anyone hiding and checking the damage."

"Did you remove your valuables when all this started?"

"I've had a storage unit and a safety deposit box for years. Nothing of real value in there." He pointed at the door.

"The life of a law officer or a detective. We make enemies." Chet's tone was ironic.

Farmington stepped out the door. "I hope you have somewhere else you can stay tonight."

"I do. Did they find the surveillance cameras?"

"Wads of gum in three of them. They may not have seen the fourth one, in that bathroom by the back door."

"Might be something useful on that one. We can hope." Farmington went back inside.

Chet pushed off from the SUV. "Do you want to take a look?"

"Sure." Doug levered himself off the car seat, putting his weight on his good leg and the cane. And limped inside.

He exhaled a big breath. His big-screen TV pulverized. His leather couch slashed. All drawers emptied onto the floor, then smashed. Tables overturned, then smashed. CDs all over the carpet, smashed. Books thrown from the bookcases. At least they weren't torn. "They must have used crowbars."

Chet spun around. "My guess too.

Doug limped into the bedroom. "No one will ever sleep on that mattress again." The slashes went all the way through the entire thickness. The dresser mirror had been smashed into tiny pieces.

"You're taking this calmly." Chet was right behind him. "Aren't you worried?"

"I'm last on Moreno's list. He's looking for Dani next."

"The daughter who flew in from Florida?"

"Yes. I can't let him find her. If I can keep them busy elsewhere, I can keep her hidden."

"Where is she now?"

"At Dave's house. Alison will be there tonight too." He bent over and picked up a shirt from the floor. His clothes were all over the floor, wrinkled but still intact. "I need to take a change of clothes with me." He glanced around.

"Point out what you want. I'll pick them up." Chet grabbed a duffel from the floor of the closet and Doug quickly had what he needed.

Chet headed for the living room, carrying the bag. "One

more thing you need to do. Park your SUV in your garage and let other people chauffeur you. You won't leave a trail that way."

Doug limped along behind him. "My car has hand controls. I can't drive anything else because my right leg is too weak."

"Use your employees as drivers."

"I can't spare enough people to keep me on the move."

"Work it out some way." Chet kicked a pillow out of the way.

"I have more to do this afternoon. I'll put the car in the garage, before I go to where I'm going to sleep." Maybe. He didn't like not having his wheels. Having to depend on someone else.

"Do you know where you'll be tonight?"

"Not at Dave's, where Dani is. Probably the extra apartment, in the building where Alison lives. I had Meagan rent another apartment this morning, just in case we needed it."

Chet pushed open the screen door. "Good thinking. You need it. Call me later and let me know the address and apartment number. I'll alert the force that we're keeping an eye on you 24/7."

Doug limped outside. "Thanks. That will help."

"Judging from what has already happened today, I'm betting this whole mess escalates fast and will be over just as fast."

Doug stopped at the SUV and Chet handed him the bag with his clothes. "That's what my gut instinct is telling me." And he didn't like how that made him feel. Out of control. Vulnerable. Scared.

THE SECURITY BUZZER SCREECHED.

Alison's heart thundered. Moreno? One of his henchmen?

She dropped the jeans she was holding and patted the holster under her arm. Of course her revolver was there.

The screech became louder, longer, more insistent and her heart nearly did a double time rhythm. Then she almost laughed. A killer wouldn't ring a doorbell.

She headed for the living room. Her hand shook when she pressed the buzzer. "Yes?"

"It's Doug. May I come up?"

Doug. Relief flooded her. But only for a moment.

Her heart rhythm went back to double time. Why was he here? Did something else happen?

"Sure." She pushed the release button to unlock the lower door. It would take him some time to get to the elevator and down the hall to her apartment on the second floor. She tried several calming breaths to quiet her rapid heartbeat. Once she got her fluttering nerves under control, she hurried back to the bathroom for her toiletries.

Then she finishing stuffing her clothes and other items into the duffel and a small suitcase. And moved everything into the living room. The tap of his cane sounded in the hallway. Then the knock on the door. She left the chain on the door and opened it wide enough to see it was only Doug. She released the chain and opened the door.

"Good. You're being cautious." Doug limped into the room, carrying a bag in his left hand.

She stood back, not offering help. He would decline any assistance from her, though he was undoubtedly hurting. He reached the couch and used his cane to lever himself down. Stoic Doug. Part of who he was. The epitome of manhood, tall, buff, handsome. But legs crippled by that car bomb.

She sat on the chair facing him. She had her own scars. Just hidden.

"I'm ready to go to Dave's." She pointed to the bags on the floor.

"Could you spare me thirty minutes and some sheets and towels?"

"What's up?"

"My house got tossed." His words held a note of exasperation, not panic.

"How bad?"

"A big message. I'm not safe at home. I'll have Scott upgrade security at all the houses and apartments."

"Are you planning to use the apartment on the third floor?"

"Until Jake gets the safe house and we figure out how to get in and out without detection."

"Do you have the door key?"

"Yes. Meagan left it at the agency before she and her family left town. But I thought it wouldn't be wise to be seen shopping for sheets and towels."

She chuckled. Not a full laugh. It wasn't a laughing matter. "I'm sure you're being watched. They know about this apartment building by now, if they didn't already."

"I'm glad you're going to Dave's." He said the words softly. "Not only for Dani, but for your own safety." She detected a tone that could be fear.

"But you'll be here by yourself."

"Only one night, maybe two." He shifted on the couch and extended his bum leg. "Safer for everyone if I'm here."

"You're not a pariah."

"I don't want anyone else to die."

A knot formed in her stomach. "Unpleasant subject. Let's get you set up." She went to the linen closet in the hallway and filled another duffel bag with a set of sheets, a light blanket, towels and wash cloths, bath soap, toothpaste, and a new toothbrush.

They took the elevator to the third floor and found the apartment. Doug unlocked the door and limped in. She followed him and glanced around. Sparsely furnished like her own apartment. A place to sleep and keep belongings. That's all she'd needed when she moved in. That's all she wanted now.

"I'll make up the bed for you." She headed to the bedroom and quickly put on the sheets and blanket, and stowed the other items in the bathroom.

He was sitting on the couch when she returned to the living room.

"You had the key. But you used the buzzer."

"To warn you I was coming."

"Cell phone?" Something in his expression puzzled her again.

"Buzzer was quicker." He stood, leaving his cane on the couch. "Thanks for all you and Scott did for my mother."

He limped toward her. That look in his eyes. She'd seen it before. But not when they were alone in an apartment. Her heartbeat sped up again, this time sparked by his scorching gaze.

She couldn't have moved if she'd wanted to. That look. The remembered feel of his hand on top of hers. He was interested. Definitely interested.

He reached out, pulled her close. His arms were strong, vise-like, yet not threatening. The scent of him teased her senses. She melted against his chest. Wanting. Waiting. She raised her head. What would it feel like to kiss him?"

He lowered his head and took her lips, gently. Drawing her in. Then deepened the kiss.

Tendrils of need scorched through her, lighting all her nerve endings. The man knew how to kiss. Yet it scared her.

Panic took over. She pushed at him. "No. No. Please don't. I'm not ready for this."

His eyes were heavy and his breath came in short little bursts. He released her. "I'm sorry. I didn't mean to upset you." He stammered the words.

"I'm confused." She pressed her hand to her chest. Her damn heart was revved up to overdrive. "I'm sorry too. I don't want to hurt you." Her heart ached, for him, for her, for what could never be.

"When this is over, we're going to talk." He reached for his cane. "I want to understand you."

"That might scare you away."

"I'll take my chances."

"I've got to go to Dave's. Dani." She rushed out of the apartment.

CHAPTER 6

*W*hat the hell was he thinking? Doug limped to his desk and booted his computer. Then stared out the window, focusing on the deep green leaves of the elm tree next to the street.

He took a deep breath. That was the problem. He wasn't thinking. He'd acted on instinct, letting his hormones overpower reason. Bad judgment. Bad timing.

His body still ached with need.

He swiveled his chair so he was facing the computer. And clicked into a database file he'd been using the day before his world had imploded on him.

Dani was safe for now, but he was especially worried about Alison. When he'd first met Alison at the firing range, she'd hinted at a rough past as a reason for learning to shoot. She was from south central L.A., a rough part of town. Must have had something to do with a man, or men. She was sure skittish.

She took some PI courses and got her license, then joined the agency. Three years ago.

And he had this strange compulsion that time was running out. He needed to move quickly. Needed to make a connection with Alison. No more standing at a distance, wondering what had happened and how she'd survived whatever it was that made her afraid of a close relationship with a man.

She didn't want to be kissed. Yet she seemed to enjoy it at first. Leaning into him. Not pushing him away.

Not right away.

The side door opened and shut again. He tensed, his shoulders rigid. Someone with a key. Alison appeared in his office doorway. Looking apprehensive. Like she was worried about her welcome.

His shoulders stayed rigid. "Come on in." He tried to smile but knew it looked forced. He wasn't in a smiling mood.

She stepped into the room. "Doug, I feel terrible. I've hurt your feelings."

"I'll live."

She settled gingerly into a chair, twisting her hands in front of her. "I didn't mean to hurt you. It's not you. It's me. The problems are inside me."

He leaned forward and kept his voice gentle. "Are you going to let them fester for the rest of your life?"

"I'm trying to forget the past. And move on."

"Completely alone? No close friends? No lovers?" Still quiet words so as not to spook her.

"That's my plan."

"I'd like to change your plan, if you give me a chance." This time he added a bit of forcefulness behind his words.

"Why?"

A simple question, but loaded with possibilities. He thought about the best way to answer. And decided on the simple truth.

"I've been intrigued by you from the first time I saw you at that shooting range."

She scooted the chair closer to the desk. "The day we met?"

"No. I'd been watching you for a couple of weeks. From the booth."

"So you knew I could shoot when you approached me that day." Not a question.

"Yes. And I knew you were a mystery woman who didn't talk to anyone at the range."

She raised her brows but didn't say anything.

"And since you've joined the agency, you've kept your personal life to yourself. You don't share stories."

She turned away. "I try not to think about what happened in Los Angeles. I came north for a fresh start." Her words were quiet.

"What if your past comes back to haunt you someday?"

Her gaze met his. "Like yours has? I'll deal with it when it happens. Like you're doing now." She looked down like she'd had a sudden thought.

"What?" He shifted on his chair.

"My past could catch up with me again. A distinct possibility. That's all."

"And you're not going to tell me what that past is that could come calling. I might be able to help you."

She shook her head but didn't say anything.

"I hope you're luckier than I've been."

"Just for the record. My reaction earlier had absolutely nothing to do with your legs. Just so you know."

She'd changed the subject. "I didn't think it did. I knew you were troubled. That was a clumsy approach. My mistake."

"I don't want to lose my job." Her gaze challenged him.

"This has nothing to do with your job. Nothing. Just one

human being wanting a deeper connection with another human being."

"Yeah...ah..."

The side door opened. Scott came in and acted surprised to see the two of them sitting there.

"I'm leaving." Alison stood. "Talk to you later, Doug." Her expression was somber. His mood plummeted.

"Tell Dani I'll call her this evening, that I wish I could be with her now."

"I'm sure she understands the risk for both of you." She left and the outside door closed with its usual thud.

At least she was still speaking to him. Would she ever trust him with her secrets?

Scott sat in the chair she'd vacated, his expression questioning.

"Is my mother's house done?" He could avoid questions too.

"She's as protected as possible."

"My house was tossed today. Don't put it on your list of future projects. I'm not going back there."

"We're all at risk."

"I know. But anyone who's still living in their own digs needs a security upgrade, no matter the cost."

"Your money." Scott stood. "I'll get on it." The outside door closed behind him.

Doug put his head in his hands. His actions years ago had put everyone he cared about in jeopardy.

THE WAIL of a siren jolted Alison. An unmarked patrol car guided the van behind her to the curb. Damn. She hadn't spotted the tail. Too absorbed in her own misery.

Guilt washed through her. She'd been thinking about Doug's kiss. Thinking about how she'd kissed him back. Thinking about the panic that took over.

She'd have to avoid any more close encounters with Doug. No repeats needed. She cared too much for him to see him hurt. She'd meant it when she told him she was going to stay alone.

Was that what she really wanted? Or was it men turning to monsters in a relationship that she feared? She shook her head. No time to think about that. She was on assignment. Protect Dani. Her personal life didn't matter.

She glanced behind her. Bless Chet for those unmarked cars.

After a stop at the grocery store, she reached Dave's house without picking up another tail.

Dave opened the door as she approached. "All okay?" His gaze was questioning.

"An unmarked car stopped my tail on Burnside. We have to be very careful."

He helped her carry the grocery bags into the house.

Dani was on the couch, watching a movie on TV. She glanced up when Alison passed by, then went back to the movie.

"Almost the end. She likes movies." Dave shrugged.

"Whatever works. We don't know how long she'll have to hide. It won't be over until Moreno himself is captured."

"Or killed." Venom dripped from his words.

Dave led the way to the kitchen and they put the food away. They'd eat dinner later. A long evening stretched before them. Dave opened a bag of tortilla chips, poured them into a bowl. Took the lid off a container of salsa, and carried them to the living room.

"I have to get my bags out of the car." Alison headed for the front door. "I wish there was somewhere I could hide the car for the night."

"I have a neighbor with an almost empty garage. He's a biker too and his bike sits on one side. I'm always kidding him that he needs to buy a car, just to use the garage. I'll call him."

With her car safely stowed out of sight two doors down, Alison settled into the chair in the living room. All her nerves still on edge. Too much had happened for one day. Her body was revved up and tense.

The movie ended, and Dani's eyes clouded with tears. Maybe that's what she needed, an emotional release.

"I'm glad you came back." Dani gestured toward the bowl of chips. "And brought snacks." Then her face sobered. "What's going on? Is my dad still okay?"

"Everyone's okay. We've been planning and plotting and someone else following me was arrested by the police."

Alarm flashed in Dani's eyes.

"Everything's under control." She shouldn't have told Dani. She kept her tone light, to smooth over her blunder. "The police and the agency are all at work."

"But I'm scared."

"Of course you are. We all are. Your sister died because of this madness. Your father has said more than once that he doesn't want anyone else to die."

"I could leave now and go to...Canada maybe."

Dave sat on the end of the couch. "No guarantee you'd be safer there. And you'd have to get there without Moreno finding out you'd left town. Too risky."

Dani scooted to the other end of the couch.

Alison hoped she could spend enough time with Dani in the days to come, since she was still uncomfortable with Dave. Was it his appearance only, or did it go deeper? This arrangement might not work.

Dave's cell phone rang. "It's Scott." He took the call.

From his side of the conversation, Alison surmised that a security system would be installed at Dave's house first thing in the morning. His house was first on the list.

When he ended the call, he stood and started pacing the floor. "This is big. Major security for all the houses."

"We're all in danger." Alison shifted in the chair. It wasn't particularly comfortable. "You got that message didn't you? They could strike out at anyone associated with Doug. Anyone they can get close to." She told him the preparations they'd made at Betty's house. And why. That Moreno had used fire-bombs down in Los Angeles against those he was targeting. Several times.

"So firebombing is possible here too. At least my house is one story."

"Dani and I will be at the back of the house." Alison stood. "Let's go look at the window situation, and figure out exits for every contingency."

They went to the bedroom. Dani followed but stood by the door, watching. Not saying anything. Alison knew she was worried. But she needed to be prepared too. All three of them might be scrambling for their lives before morning.

Dave pulled back the drapes, exposing the latches that kept the window locked. It was an older home with old-fashioned window locks. "You have to unlatch this and push up the window." He demonstrated. "Then push out the screen. It's easy to remove. Too easy. I don't sleep with the windows open. I use the air conditioner during the summer. That's why it's on now."

"I'm glad I live on the second floor." Alison let go of the drape she'd pulled back. "But I still won't open my window."

"In Florida we kept windows open." Dani's words carried a note of panic. "Guess it wasn't safe."

"Nothing is completely safe." Alison gazed around the small room, at the bed, the closet door, that one window. "All we can do is prepare and hope for the best."

Dave relocked the window and pulled the drapes closed. "The security system will be installed tomorrow morning. If nothing happens tonight, we'll be safer tomorrow night."

CHAPTER 7

*D*oug shut off his computer, grabbed his cane and briefcase. He was ready to leave for the evening. Tomorrow he'd have someone move his computer into the conference room. He glanced at the window, at the blind he'd pulled down while he worked.

The doorbell on the side door buzzed. He was alone. Erik had left ten minutes earlier after taking care of all the back-ups. So his car would be the only one outside. He needed a security camera outside the door with a feed to his office and the conference room. Something else for Scott to handle.

He limped to the outer door. "Who's there?" He shouted loud enough for his voice to penetrate the thick door.

"It's Nick. Open up."

Doug unlocked the door and limped back to his office. Nick followed.

"Where's Tricia? Why aren't you with her?" Doug settled into his desk chair.

Nick sat. "She's hiding out with a friend in Salem. Staying away from our house."

"How's that going to keep her safe?" His mind flashed to an image of Roger Mobley, dead on the floor, and he shuddered.

"I'm making arrangements to hire a private detective with no ties to this agency to stay with her at all times. I have to work this case."

"What if that baby comes early? Then she goes to a hospital, unprotected."

"The detective can stay at the hospital too. Tricia's idea. Besides, she's still a month away from her due date."

"I still don't like it."

"I should have the detective in place by morning. Tricia knows I can't sit home with her, and let the rest of you risk your lives with Moreno and his hoods."

"I still think your place is with her."

"What if Moreno knows where we live? As your niece she could be a target too."

"You could have taken time off and taken her out of town." He snapped out the words.

"No. I'm a member of the task force. A cop. A detective. My place is here, helping to protect you and Dani and the rest of the agency people. And stop Moreno."

"And Tricia is okay with that?"

"She's more concerned about little Emily. She wanted to get herself and her unborn daughter out of town to a safer place."

Uneasiness settled into him. Decisions being made involving family without his knowledge.

Nick stood. "And now let's you and I go grab some dinner. I'm betting you don't have anything to eat at that apartment and you don't need to go grocery shopping by yourself tonight."

"Who's idea was that?"

"Chet and I discussed it. Let's go. Drive your car and follow me to that grill on 23rd. I'm ready for a steak." As much as he wanted to say no, he was hungry and Nick was right. He'd be a target out on the street by himself. He stood and picked up his briefcase again.

They settled into a booth at a restaurant not far from the office.

Doug stretched out his leg to ease the ache. "Explain something to me. Why do I have keepers now?"

Nick laughed. "We watch out for each other. Isn't that how it's always worked?"

"But you're making decisions for me. I want to call the shots."

"Not going to happen. Chet's orders. Chet, Jake, and I had a lunch meeting today. Task force business. This operation is out of your hands. We're going to coordinate efforts and protect you, whether you like it or not."

He glared at Nick.

The waitress took their order. They both knew what they wanted without looking at a menu. This was a favorite agency hangout. And they served great steaks. And great hamburgers. He agreed with Nick. Tonight was steak night.

When the waitress filled their coffee cups and left the table, Doug returned to his interrupted train of thought. "I don't like it. This business of someone else telling me what to do and where to go. I'm armed, as usual."

"But you can't run fast. Someone else needs to be with you at all times, except tonight while you're sleeping, and possibly tomorrow night. We're hoping for that big of a window of time."

"Yeah, they've already hit my house. Dani is the primary target right now. Until he discovers he can't get to her."

"Chet said Moreno told you he was saving you for last. Nice of him to give us that much information."

"Everyone around me is at risk, though. Including you."

Nick winced. "I know. You saved my life and Jack's by shooting Moreno's sons."

"Moreno knows too. You can count on it."

Their salads arrived and they started eating.

Doug put down his fork. "Moreno was boasting when he told me his plan. Isolate me, then move in for the kill."

"He probably thinks you're weak now. We'll spoil his game every chance we get. We have one of his goons in jail on charges of illegal entry into the country, and driving without a license or insurance. That will hold him a few days while he's being questioned. Then he can be turned over to the INS, if we can't find anything else to stick him with."

"What was he doing?"

"Tailing Alison on the way to Dave's. The call you made to Chet. The guy protested, of course, when he was pulled over. No license. No insurance. So he was arrested and his status checked. He had a picture of Alison's Taurus on his cell phone."

A chill went up his spine. "If Alison hadn't spotted him, they'd know where Dani is." He didn't like close calls.

"Everyone gets an unmarked patrol car as an escort till this is over."

"Good." At least that part of the problem was solved.

Their steaks arrived. When they finished eating and they pushed their plates away, the waitress refilled their coffee cups.

Nick picked up his cup and took a sip, then set it down. "We'll get Dani out of Dave's on Monday. Jake gets the keys to the house that morning. Then the furniture rental company will deliver the furniture he picked out today. After that people can move in. Anyone who wants or needs to."

Doug didn't like it that he hadn't been in on the planning with Jake. But he tamped down his anger and feelings of helplessness. "Dave can't take Dani to the house. He doesn't have a car. Alison can do that." At least he had something to offer.

"Or someone else Moreno hasn't targeted yet."

"You're right. She's had a tail. Who hasn't?"

"Rafe or Scott or Kara?"

"Any one of them." Doug picked up his coffee and sipped. He'd let it cool down too much. Something else to annoy him.

Nick signaled the waitress for another warm up. "The way things have been set up with the house, Dani should be safe there. Surrounded by more people. Now it's just Dave, or Dave and Alison."

"We need Alison's shooting skills wherever we're sleeping."

"Those in the house will sleep in shifts so someone is always awake and alert."

He gazed at Nick. "Just for the record. What haven't you told me yet? That guarded expression of yours tells me you're holding back."

He laughed. "You always could read me. We have one more thing to do this evening. We're going to take your car and put it in your garage, then I'm going to drive you to the apartment building."

"Wait a minute. You can't take my car away from me." An angry knot built in his gut.

"It's a dead giveaway. Moreno's men know what you drive and that you can't run. You're a sitting duck all alone in the car."

"I'll feel even more helpless than I am." That knot tied tighter.

"We know you're not helpless. But you're always going to have someone with you when you're on the move. Until this is

52

over." This time his expression was one of dogged deter-
mination.

"Isn't there some other way?"

"No. In the morning, I'll pick you up for breakfast. Then
we'll meet Chet and Jake at the motel where Jake is staying. Jake
won't go to the office. He'll run his end of the task force business from the safe house."

That angry knot burned like fire in his gut. "I don't like
being without my car. That's taking this protection thing
too far."

BY MORNING DOUG had cooled down. The protector had
become the protected. A role he had to accept. Until Moreno
was in jail.

But he didn't have to like it.

If he were killed, he couldn't protect Dani. Or get to know
her. That's what he wanted, more than anything else. To get
acquainted with this young woman who happened to be his
long lost daughter.

Okay, he could cooperate, up to a point. But when he could,
he'd take back control. He was head of the agency under attack.
He was the main target.

He limped to the couch in the living room, waiting for
Nick's call that he was out front.

After breakfast Nick drove across the river to a motel near
the Lloyd Center and easily found Jake's room. He knocked and
Jake opened the door. Chet was already there.

Doug limped in, cane in hand. Jake had four chairs grouped
around a small table in the center of the room. A laptop sat

open in the middle of the table. He made a mental note. Carry his laptop. Act like a leader.

Jake greeted them, then gestured toward the chairs. "Take a seat."

Doug sat, stretching out his aching right leg. "Any developments?"

"That guy in the van that was following Alison tried to play dumb and pretend he didn't understand English." Chet grinned. "Nick and I grilled him all night, taking turns going at him."

"He broke about five am and started talking," Nick said. "He doesn't want to be sent back to Mexico. But he also knows his life isn't worth anything now. Moreno doesn't keep guys who get busted."

And Nick hadn't told him at breakfast. "Well, what did he say?" Doug let his impatience come through in his voice.

"Moreno is somewhere in a house in the hills," Chet said. "Out in the country. Not Portland. Armando is with him."

"Armando. The older son. Born in L.A. but raised in Mexico."

"The only son you didn't kill in that raid." Nick scowled. "He came with Moreno when he returned to L.A. last year."

"The mistress's son. Born before Moreno married." Doug had heard about the son, but had never seen him.

"That's the one," Nick said. "Before Eddie Velasquez died, he said Armando was calling himself El Diablo. Do we know what his full legal name is?"

Jake stood and reached for the coffees on the dresser. "I'll find out. I do know that this son has a mean streak that comes from clawing his way up in the cartel. Anyone who opposed him disappeared. He'll cause trouble for his father before this is over." Jake set a coffee cup in front of each of them. "Chet brought these."

Doug lifted his cup in salute. "Has that guy you questioned been to the place in the country? Does he know where it is?"

"He claims he doesn't and he could be telling the truth," Chet said. "Moreno is cautious. Takes no chances."

Nick picked up his cup. "Which means there is another place where gang members are hanging out."

"Then we have to locate that house and the house in the country. Follow someone instead of arrest them." Doug shifted in his chair, trying not to let on how much his leg was hurting him today. That bed had not been comfortable.

"First we have to figure out how to spot Moreno's boys before we can follow them and find the hideout," Nick said. "Any ideas?"

"Oregon has a high Hispanic population," Chet said. "Some are American citizens. Some are migrant workers from Mexico, here legally. Some are illegals."

"Moreno's boys could be any of the groups. Drug money can corrupt good people." Jake's tone reeked of disgust. Doug had to agree with him.

Chet took a sip of his coffee and sat back. "I'm putting more patrols out to watch for tails and to be ready to follow anyone who acts suspicious. We might get lucky and someone will head to the hideout."

"We may not have that much time." Nick turned to Doug. "What are you planning to do today? Are you going to the office? Will others be there?"

"What? You're not going to babysit me the rest of the day?" His words dripped with sarcasm.

Nick glared at him. "You're on your own as soon as I drop you off. Your people will be your transportation and protection. I'll be doing task force business."

Doug's gut instinct kicked into high gear. The undertones in the room spoke volumes. What was going on? "I've asked Erik and Rafe to come to the office to run some data searches. Maybe find a link to some of Moreno's group." And give him something to do besides stare at four walls. He was used to keeping busy. Didn't like waiting around for something to happen.

"Wish we had the house already," Jake said. "Then we could hang out and spend a lazy Sunday. I have a flat screen TV coming tomorrow."

"Where's the house located?" Doug didn't like being the last one to find out.

"On East Burnside." Jake turned on his laptop. "I'll show you on Google Earth. It's a huge corner lot, lots of trees, hedges, bushes. You can't see much from the street."

Once he had the image up, he rotated the laptop so Doug could see it. "The driveway on the right side of the property is wide and curves around to the back, giving us plenty of room for parking. There's a garage straight back, but we don't have to use it. Safer not to."

"What other access?" Doug leaned closer.

"A gate to the back of the house, located on a narrow side street. We'll need someone at the back of the house on watch."

"And someone with a view of the front and the driveway, so you can see who comes in and out," Chet said.

"We'll keep two people on watch duty at all times. One slip and they'll know where we are. I'm beginning to think the big house for everyone is a bad idea." Doug didn't like deciding he'd made a wrong decision in agreeing to put everyone in one place. But that's the way he felt today.

"Strength in numbers," Nick said.

"Big target. But I want to be where my daughter is. So we'll find a way to make it work."

"I'll let you know when the furniture is in place," Jake said. "Then people can start trickling in."

"Are you guys going to keep me informed of what's going on?" Doug gazed at each man in turn. "What progress you're making to catch Moreno and put him in jail?"

Jake turned off the computer and stood. Chet and Nick returned his gaze without comment.

"What aren't you telling me?"

"Nothing." Jake's reply was curt.

CHAPTER 8

*A*lison paced the hallway of the agency, waiting for Doug. Surely he wouldn't stay by himself in that apartment all day.

She couldn't believe her dumb luck. Kenny was getting out of prison this week. That call from her lawyer couldn't have come at a worse time.

A blast of pain penetrated her heart. She needed to go into hiding. Leave the agency. Leave town. Leave Doug. She'd miss him.

A car pulled into the lot at the side of the building. She stopped her pacing and stepped into the conference room. The side door opened and the unmistakable tap of Doug's cane echoed in the hallway. Nick followed him in the door.

"Alison?" Nick called out.

"I'm here." She stopped in the doorway to the conference room.

"I thought you told me Erik and Rafe were working this morning." Nick's tone was accusing.

"Maybe I'm early. We didn't set an exact time."

"Don't take such chances. Make sure you're not alone where Moreno's men can get to you."

"I'll stay until Erik and Rafe come," Alison said. "I need to talk to Doug."

"Okay. I'm on my way. I was up all night. I need sleep." Nick went out the side door.

"What was he doing?" Alison followed Doug into his office.

"He and Chet interrogated the guy in the van who tailed you." Doug closed the blinds, then sat in his chair. "Didn't get much, but we know there's a place in the country where Moreno is hiding and Armando is with him."

She sat in front of the desk, glad for the barrier between them. What she had to say was too personal for him to be close. She'd have to tell him enough about Kenny so he wouldn't stop her from leaving.

"We should be in the conference room. Just in case." He stood. "Safety first." He picked up his briefcase.

"You're not counting on Moreno saving you for last?" She reached for the briefcase and he handed it to her.

"I'm not counting on anything anymore." He picked up his laptop. "I want to know what that task force is supposed to be doing. I'm not sure capturing Moreno quickly is their objective."

"Why not?"

"That's what I want to know." He grabbed his cane and limped across the hall to the conference room.

She followed. "If Armando is here too, that means big trouble. Velasquez said he was ruthless. He's the enforcer, the executioner."

He chose a chair across the table from the door and set his cane and laptop on the table before sitting down. "You got more information in L.A. than I thought. Why haven't we talked about this?"

She sat across from him. Still keeping distance between them. "I figured you knew. I knew Velasquez was talking to Nick and passing on information, before Moreno found out and had him killed."

"We lost a good informant when he died. Do you know Armando's full name? We only know the Armando part. Don't know if he uses the surname Moreno. His mother was never married to Ramon Moreno."

"I've never heard his full name. Erik ought to be able to find it for you, when he gets here."

"Jake said he'd find out, but I'll have Erik search too. Armando is calling himself El Diablo."

"His ties to the cartel are strong. That I do know."

"Now, what did you want to talk about?" He asked the question with a quirk of an eyebrow. Looking a bit self-conscious, like she was going to bring up that kiss again.

"I got a call from my lawyer in L.A. My ex, Kenny Driscoll, is getting out of San Quentin in a few days. He'll be coming after me, to kill me." She blurted it out. Just the bare facts. "I need to leave town. Now, before he gets here."

"Why?" Just the one word. Quiet but forceful.

"I shot him in the shoulder in self-defense and he went to prison for assault." She lifted her chin, keeping her gaze on him. She needed all the inner strength she could find deep down inside.

"Where would you go? How would you hide where he couldn't find you?"

"I don't know. I just know I have to go. Now." She rushed the words.

"How do you know he's planning to come after you?" Doug's tone was quiet, soothing almost.

An involuntary shudder wracked her body. "His parting words to me were, 'I'm going to find you and cut you to ribbons when I get out.'"

"He likes knives?"

Remembered pain slashed through her. "A wicked switchblade is his weapon of choice. It doesn't make the noise a gun does. Inflicts damage slowly." She held his gaze until he looked away.

"He cut you. More than once." Not a question. He got it.

"I have the scars."

"The sleeves you always wear." He'd noticed.

"The night I shot him in the shoulder he'd already broken my left arm in two places. I have surgical scars from that too. He went to prison after a stay in the hospital." Her voice quivered.

Doug leaned back, gazing at her intently. "I know this sounds illogical, but now is a good time for him to come. You're going to be surrounded by other people at all times. He's not going to get to you."

"He's being paroled. He'll be breaking his parole coming up here. But he's the type who doesn't care. He'll risk everything to get even with me."

"Another person bent on revenge."

"Maybe I'll go to Canada. Far away."

"Please don't go. And I'm not just saying this because I like having you around. I'm saying it because you need friends now. More than ever."

"He might do something crazy. He used to have an assault rifle. He may get another one." Panic laced her voice.

"When does he get out?"

"In a couple of days. Kenny called my lawyer from San Quentin and told him to tell me he's coming. Boasted that he'll get me, wherever I am." She stood and paced. Too nervous to sit still.

"What was he convicted of?"

"Aggravated assault and attempted murder."

"Okay, promise me something," Doug said. "Promise me you won't go running off today or tomorrow. Wait until we have more information on him and the restrictions on his parole. Nick can get that information. I'll call him and get him on it."

"What good will that do?" She grasped the back of the chair. Leaned toward him.

"They may be able to arrest him for parole violation before he finds you. We'll all have your back. Just like you have mine."

"You think he can be stopped?"

"Yes. Trust us, please. Stay."

"I want to stay. I don't want to run away from my responsibilities."

"Remember, you're a different person than you were when you married him." That quiet, soothing tone again.

"Yes, I am. I let the old fears resurface."

She sat in the chair and leaned toward him. "This means more risk for you, if I stay and he comes."

"I'm willing to take that chance. I don't want you leaving. I might never see you again."

She looked into his eyes and saw a man who believed in her and her strength. Even when she didn't.

"Okay. I'll stay." But if something happened to Doug because of her, she'd never forgive herself.

∼

DOUG'S CELL phone ring tone jolted him awake. Tight bands squeezed his heart. He glanced at the clock. Just after midnight. He sat up and grabbed the phone. Chet.

"Your mother's house was firebombed. I'm heading there now."

Those tight bands threatened to squeeze his heart into pieces. His hand shook and he almost dropped the phone. "My mother? Did she get out?" He flipped on the light next to the bed.

"I don't know yet. I'll call you as soon as I find out. Stay where you are. That's an order. They'll be watching for you, which is probably why her house was the target. They don't know where you are."

"I want to know if she's all right." His pounding heart was all he could hear. His mind was a muddle. He couldn't think straight.

"Of course you do. I'll get the fire chief on the phone and let him know the situation."

"Thanks."

"Gotta go. I'll be in touch." Chet ended the call.

Doug bolted from the bed and put too much weight on his right leg. It buckled, and he collapsed to the floor. He used the bed to pull himself back up and sat on the edge of the mattress. His leg throbbed. He'd never felt so helpless.

The cell phone. She had one. He located her number and dialed. No answer. It went to voice mail. He waited for the tone. "Call me. Please call me. Let me know you're okay." Desperation rode his words. Nothing he could do. He hung up.

Maybe she couldn't hear the phone. Why didn't he warn her to keep the phone handy and call at the first sign of trouble? She was too damned independent for her own good.

And he was stuck where he was. Unfamiliar room. Unfamiliar bed. Unfamiliar noises.

He couldn't do anything but wait. He was almost sorry he'd told Chet to call him immediately if anything happened. Now he had to deal with the uncertainty. Was the firebomb thrown in the front window? Did the rope ladder get her to safety? He wanted to know now. But he couldn't go to her house even if he wanted to. His car was in the garage at his house, several miles away.

He couldn't go back to sleep until he knew for sure his mother was safe. He dressed in his usual day clothes of Dockers and T-shirt. Long sleeves for the chilly night temperature. Then sat on the couch with his phone in his lap. Starring at nothing. The only light came from a small bulb in the hallway.

An agonizing thirty minutes later Chet called again.

"She got out, using the ladder. It's hanging down to the ground. She's nowhere around. No one is home at the neighbor's behind her, where she told Alison she could go."

"Damn. And she's not answering her cell phone."

"Keep calling. Let me know if you find out anything. We'll keep looking too."

"Okay." He ended the call and tried his mother's phone again. And again. And again.

CHAPTER 9

*D*oug's gut clenched into knots. He'd lost count of how many tries he'd made to call his mother. Three hours had passed since the first call from Chet. Three agonizing hours. And he didn't have coffee to help him cope.

He picked up the cell phone again and tapped the number. Voice mail. He left another curt message, "Call me." Then stared at the phone. Those knots in his gut couldn't get much tighter.

The phone rang. He jumped and almost dropped it. Her number. He answered.

"Doug, I'm sorry I didn't call you. I forgot the phone was in the backpack. I just heard the phone ring when I went to the bedroom to try to get some sleep." She sounded contrite.

"I've been worried. You should have remembered. You should have called." He kept his tone neutral despite an urge to yell at her.

"I've been talking to Jeanette, in the kitchen. I'm at her house in Beaverton."

"How did you get there?"

"My neighbor brought me. I was so scared. I climbed down that ladder like Alison showed me. I ran to the back fence, to the gate. Sue, my neighbor, brought me here." She was babbling now, almost incoherent.

Guilt welled up inside Doug, eating at his gut. "I'm glad you're safe. It's my fight with Moreno. I'm sorry he made you a target."

"I can stay here with Jeanette. After Alison and Scott left on Saturday, I took two suitcases of clothes and shoes to my neighbor's house, just in case."

He smiled despite his worry. Clothes and shoes. Okay, she was thinking ahead. Planning. His very efficient mother. "Good for you. I'm glad you took the threat seriously."

"Do you know how bad the fire was? How much was burned?" This time her voice cracked a bit. She did love her house.

"No. I'm waiting for more word from Chet, the detective who's watching out for all of us." He grabbed a pen and pad that sat next to his laptop on the coffee table. "Give me the address and home phone number for Jeanette's house. And her last name."

He wrote down the information.

"Where are you? Are you in a dangerous place too?" That cracking voice again.

"I'm hiding in an apartment building. I can't stay at my house or drive my car until this is over."

"Oh. It really is serious. I was being silly."

"Yes, it's serious. I'll be moving into a house on East Burnside later today, with some of my agency people. And Dani."

"Poor Dani. How's she holding up?"

"She's scared, of course. But she's being protected. I'll call you later. Get some sleep. Take care and stay inside."

"I will. I'm scared now." She ended the call.

And he was scared for all of them. His family and his friends. They were all targets because of him. Because he shot two low life scum who'd been shooting at him. Five years ago.

He called Chet and told him his mother was safe for now.

The security buzzer screeched. Doug woke from his nap on the couch and glanced at the clock. Barely an hour had gone by.

He went to the door and the intercom. "Who's there?"

"It's Chet. With coffee."

"Good. I'm buzzing you in."

He grabbed his cane and waited by the door until he heard a light tap, then opened the door for Chet. And snatched a coffee cup out of one hand.

"I needed this." He closed and locked the door. "Alison will be here later to pick me up for breakfast."

Chet settled into the overstuffed chair. "Nick clued me in on your addiction."

"Yeah, he's learned." Doug sank down on the couch again and turned on the lamp. The only other light in the room came through the window, spilling early morning shadows across the floor.

"Alison and Scott did a good job telling your mother what to do. She got down that rope ladder and to the neighbor's without a problem. I talked to the neighbor after she returned home from taking your mother to Beaverton."

"But now she's burned out and she's lost practically everything."

"Not everything. The fire department was there within ten minutes. The house is not a total loss."

"It was a lovely home. I was a teenager when my parents bought it." He sipped at the hot coffee. To make it last. To get the caffeine hit he needed.

"The house can be renovated. No real structural damage. The gun safe in the basement held nicely. It was completely away from the flames, back in a corner. What's in there should be okay."

"She should have gone on vacation. Then her house might have been left alone." That guilt again, gnawing at his gut.

"Maybe not. This was a warning. A big one. We have to heed it." Chet's penetrating gaze magnified his own warning. Be careful.

He got it.

He finished off his coffee and set the cup on the coffee table.

"I should have brought the whole pot."

Doug smiled. Chet's deadpan way of saying things always amused him. Yet Chet was the smartest detective he'd ever known. "So true. I'll make up for it at breakfast and when I get to the office."

"The office will be safe enough for now. As long as you have other people with you. Kara will relieve Alison at Dave's before she comes here."

"You know more than I do." And it irritated him. Yet he wasn't sure why. "You told Alison what happened?"

"We're keeping all of you in the loop. And keeping tabs on where you are at all times."

"And watching for tails?"

"We're counting on the unmarked police cars to spot all tails and get them out of circulation. One gang member at a time."

"That might work. But all it takes is one tail missed."

"It has to work. I told the chief we need perfection in this operation."

"We need that perfection as we move people into Jake's house today. Anyone who's in danger can stay at Jake's house.

I'll go later, when I leave the office. When someone can take me. Dani can be moved in whenever Alison is ready to go."

"Just for the record. I don't like the idea of a bunch of you under one roof."

"The DEA set this up. I don't like it either, but we'll make it work. We have to." His gut wrenched tighter.

Chet set his empty cup on the floor by his chair. "I heard from Jake a little while ago. Armando's full name is Armando Vidal Moreno Padilla. And he's definitely calling himself El Diablo."

"So the El Diablo name is to set himself apart from his father, since he carries his surname. His mother was Moreno's mistress before he married the mother of the sons I shot."

"Armando could have plans to be bigger and meaner than his father," Chet said. "He was raised in Mexico, not America. And had direct contact with at least one major cartel. Moreno brought him to Los Angeles when he came back to rebuild, mainly because of his cartel contacts."

"And now he trusts him with helping build the Oregon drug empire?" Doug let his tone relay his disgust.

"The Mexican drug gangs tend to rely on family and friends. And pay them well for their loyalty." Chet picked up the empty coffee cup and stood. "I need to go."

"One more problem has come up," Doug said. "Alison has an ex who's getting out of San Quentin in a few days and says he's coming for her, with a switchblade. His name is Kenny Driscoll. He's in for aggravated assault and attempted murder."

"Paroled?"

"Yes."

"So we need to be on the lookout for this guy too?"

"Yes. I did let Nick know. Can you get a mug shot? And find out the terms of his parole?"

"He'll be an added complication."

"I know. Alison wanted to leave town and go hide some-where else. I told her to stay, that she'd be better off with friends and extra protection."

"Okay," Chet said. "We'll get him for parole violation if he shows. And send him back to prison."

"Catch him, before he finds Alison and carries out his threats." He cringed as images surfaced of what a switchblade could do to Alison's flesh.

ALISON USED her key to open the security door at the apart-ment building. Then took the elevator to the third floor. She'd called from downstairs so Doug would know she was coming up.

She knocked on his door and he opened it immediately, cane in hand.

He limped into the hallway, carrying a briefcase in his left hand. She reached out and he handed her the briefcase without hesitation. He must be hurting.

He headed for the elevator. "I'm hungry. I'm not used to being in a place where there aren't any snacks or coffee."

"Well, darn. We've been neglecting you." She tried for thick sarcasm and got a smile from Doug. Rare these days.

Doug directed her to the coffee shop where he'd had break-fast with Nick the day before. They took the booth at the back.

Doug drank about half his cup of coffee before he set it down. She'd have to remember his caffeine addiction and keep it handy for him, when they all got to Jake's house. When had she started thinking in terms of taking care of him? *Careful, girl. You're stepping over the line there.*

They kept the conversation light and what she'd term normal, until after they'd eaten and their plates were removed.

Once their coffee cups were refilled, Doug pierced her with a gaze that told her it was serious time. He had something on his mind.

"If I'm going to help you, I need more information on Kenny Driscoll."

She took a deep breath. How much more should she tell him? What secrets should she continue to keep? Whatever she said wouldn't reflect well on her. She'd made some foolish choices.

She decided on a direct approach, meeting his gaze. "I was living with a guy who turned out to be a drug dealer, a big time trafficker. I hadn't seen the signs. Just knew he had money and seemed like a nice guy. Until he got physical. And wanted to hook me on drugs and send me out on the street as my pimp. I didn't have much self-esteem in those days. Kenny rescued me. My knight in shining armor."

She hesitated.

"Go on." His face showed no emotion. He was the detective listening to the story of a witness, but he wasn't taking notes.

"Kenny turned out to be even meaner than Joe. He beat me, cut me, kept me isolated. I couldn't have any friends."

"What about family?"

Another hesitation. She had to tell the truth. Get it all out. This was Doug she was talking to. "My mother was a prostitute and heroin addict. Her pimp had controlled her life. When I was eight, I was taken from her and put in foster care."

Doug's expression hadn't changed. Still in detective mode, waiting for her to continue.

She took a deep breath. "I was twelve when I was told my mother had died of a heroin overdose."

Doug flinched. "That must have been difficult, losing your mother like that." Compassion in his words.

She lifted her chin and continued to gaze directly at him, at his sympathetic brown eyes. "What I wanted most from my mother, I never got. A hug that told me she cared. I was the unwanted nuisance. I was better off in foster care."

He stared at her for a long moment. "And you've made a good life for yourself. Back to Kenny."

The waitress appeared with the coffee pot and refilled their cups.

She waited until they were alone again, her gut twisting into knots. She hated reliving those nightmares. Would he still think she was intelligent and able to hold down her job if she told him the whole truth?

"Kenny was okay for a while. Like Joe had been at first. But Kenny was a controller. I decided to leave. One day while he was at work, I went looking for a job. He found me that night at a shelter and pulled a knife and forced me to go with him."

"And no one tried to stop him? Called the police?"

"No." She sipped her coffee, getting up the nerve to go on, to get to the worst part. Doug waited patiently. Not rushing her.

"Of course Kenny became more violent after that. He started cutting on me for sport. I have scars on my back, my buttocks, my breasts. Where they aren't visible when I'm wearing clothes."

Doug reached across the table and enclosed her hand in his. A life line. "He was a master manipulator. I know his kind. I've rescued women in your position."

"I started stashing money, anything I could from the cash he gave me to buy groceries and other things. It took a long time, but when I had enough, I bought a gun."

Doug's eyebrow quirked up but he didn't say anything.

"I'd never shot a gun. I bought ammo too, and went back to the apartment."

"You should have used the money to leave again."

"Yes. But I was too afraid. He'd told me he'd kill me if I left. That night he accused me of going to see someone. He knew I'd gone out."

"The big fight?"

"Yes. He broke my left arm in two places and punched me in the face several times. This time he didn't care that the injuries showed. He started waving his knife around, telling me he was going to slice up my face, then kill me. When I got the chance, I grabbed the gun from where I'd hidden it under the bed, propped it on a pillow, and fired. I hit him in the shoulder. He dropped the knife."

"Did you run then?"

"I didn't have to. The police were pounding on the door. The neighbors had heard my screams and called 911. We were both taken to the hospital and he was put under arrest for aggravated assault and attempted murder."

"And now he's getting out and he's after revenge." Doug shook his head. "What a sorry excuse for a man. I'd like to get my hands on him."

"I don't know what he'll do if he finds me. If he'll have the knife like he said. Or if he'll have a gun."

"You're not going to be alone again until he's back behind bars. I told Chet to get a mug shot and find out the terms of his parole."

A mug shot. One more confession to make. "Kenny's mother was Hispanic. His father was part Hispanic. He looks like he could fit in with Moreno's men."

CHAPTER 10

When Alison pulled away from the coffee shop, Doug spotted the tail behind them. Someone he knew from Los Angeles. He'd sent Enrique to prison for a couple of years during his early detective days.

"Pull up beside that unmarked car." He pointed to a nondescript brown sedan. Alison stopped and Doug lowered his window. "That blue car behind us. Enrique Herrera, Moreno's cousin." He motioned for Alison to go on.

The unmarked patrol car pulled Enrique over. "Tail is gone."

Alison laughed. "It helps to know who we're up against."

Alison pulled into the parking lot at the agency. Erik's car was the only one there. When they got inside, Erik was in the conference room, on his computer.

Doug leaned over his shoulder. "What do you have?"

Erik gestured toward the screen. "Database records on Mexican cartel connections. I got lucky. A reporter friend of mine gave me the password for access."

"Terrific. Anything good yet?"

Erik turned around. "No. Moreno has a lot of relatives, but no one we've identified here yet."

"Enrique Herrera was our tail this morning. He was pulled over after we came out of the coffee shop."

"Nice break. I'll look for ties to him. Moreno's wife's sister's son, right?"

"That's the one."

"He has a sister who's deep into the drug gangs. A frequent mule, bringing in shipments from Mexico, taking back the cash to the cartel."

"You're doing good, Erik. Keep looking." Doug limped into his own office and set his briefcase down.

Alison followed him. "What can I do to help? I'm not just a hired gun."

Doug laughed and leaned against the edge of his desk. "Come here. Push that door closed first."

She gave him a questioning look, but closed the door and came to him, standing in front of him. Just out of reach.

"Closer."

She stepped closer.

"He reached out and pulled her into his arms. "I want to give you a hug. That's all. Just a hug." He kept his words quiet, soothing.

She melted against him. Her scent teasing his nostrils. The warmth of her breasts pressed to his chest threatened his resolve to settle for just a hug.

She started to pull away. He tightened his hold.

"I want to hold you for a minute. You took a big chance today. You trusted me with information you've never told anyone else."

She squirmed and he released her. She stepped back and her gaze caught his. "Thanks. I think." She smiled, an embarrassed smile, like she wasn't sure she'd done the right thing. "I'll see if I can help Erik with the records." She glanced at the window behind him. "You should be in the conference room too."

"As soon as I take care of something I need to do in here."

She frowned at him, then left the office.

Had he started something he shouldn't? He was fourteen years older than she was, and had been married twice. And she had a muddled past and wasn't willing to trust him yet with complete information. Though he knew a lot more now than he did before her confession this morning. She did need tenderness and love. Could he give it to her? His runaway libido signaled that he should. Yet…he could lose her too.

First Moreno. And Kenny. Then he'd explore the connection between them.

He limped behind his desk and sat in his chair. Work time. He booted his computer and took his laptop and a flash drive out of his briefcase. He'd made some notes the night before on his laptop, and had copied them to his flash drive. He needed to synchronize his files. He'd have Erik move his computer into the conference room later.

Scott came through the door. "Do you have time for me to give you an update?"

"Always time for your reports. How many crews are out today?"

Scott laughed. "Three crews are working. They should be able to do all the houses today, including Jake's safe house. His landlord said okay, if the improvements are left when he moves out. The apartments are trickier. We need permission from out of state owners."

"The apartment building where Alison lives should be secure." Doug grimaced. "I hope. They have their own cameras in the entrance area. And a buzzer system to get inside."

"Erik's apartment is going to be the troublesome one. California landlord. Managed by a company that isn't keen on problems."

"Well, do what you can. Some security is better than none. This may be over fast, or it may drag on. I'm thinking fast. Moreno was always high energy, raring to go."

"I'll get on it." Scott left.

Doug got up and closed the door. That was a sign he was working on something and wanted to be left alone for a while. He picked up his phone and called three local hotels he did business with regularly. Whenever he wanted to stash someone in a safe place. He reserved a suite in each hotel, under the business name he used for such emergencies. The hotels were always happy to accommodate him and his people.

Then he called Sidney, his mechanic. The man who did all the work on his cars. The man who stored his old car with the hand controls, as a backup. Sid came to the phone.

"Hey, Sid. Doug Landreth. I have two very important requests. I'm having a problem with a drug dealer who wants me dead."

"I don't take out drug dealers." Sid's tone was deadpan.

Doug laughed. "I wish you could. Hey, I need that Subaru of mine out of storage. I need a different car with hand controls. And my SUV, in my garage at my house, needs to go into storage for a while. The gang knows that vehicle but not the Subaru."

"Sure. I can do the switch for you. I'll need the key to the garage and the SUV."

"I'm at the office. Pick up the keys here. And park the Subaru up the side street several houses up. Far enough it won't be hit in a shootout."

"You're serious, aren't you?"

"Yeah. This jerk had my younger daughter killed last Thursday."

"Damn. I'll get right on it. I'll check out the Subaru and fill it with gas and have it to you by eleven."

"You're a good man, Sid. I knew I could count on you." He ended the call, then silently congratulated himself. Paying to keep that old car in storage had given him one more option in this game he seemed to be playing with Moreno and his gang. He wasn't going to be without wheels after all. And Moreno didn't know about the other car. It had been in storage for three years.

Later today he'd have someone take him back to his house to pack up the things that would upset him if they were lost. There wasn't much left after Moreno's boys smashed up the place. But he had a few keepsakes that might not have been touched. And books, lots of books. The CDs and DVDs were mostly gone. He had a funny feeling that his house might be the next target. The next blatant warning.

ALISON PEEKED AROUND THE CORNER. Doug's door was open again, after that mechanic left. Her curiosity aroused, she finished with the file she was searching and closed down the computer. And went into Doug's office.

"What was Sidney doing here?"

"I'll tell you if you won't report to Chet or Nick." He said it with a grin but she knew he was serious.

He was up to something. He seemed more cheerful and upbeat. Like he'd figured out a puzzle and was proud of himself.

"I don't work for them. I work for you."

He stared at her for a few moments. "Good enough for me.

Sid is bringing me my old Subaru and parking it up the street, in case I need to make a quick getaway. He also took the SUV out of my garage and put it in storage, until this is over."

"You have been busy. Now what? I have a feeling there's more." She could tell by his mood. He was back to commander mode. Doing the kinds of things he'd been trained to do. Organize and implement.

He laughed. "You're learning how to read me. Yes, I feel more in control today than I did yesterday. Now I have one more bit of preparation but I'll need a driver."

"Okay. What do you want to do?"

"Go to my house and pack up anything else I don't want destroyed, what's left that is."

"And?"

"Put them in my storage unit. Alert your police tail. I don't want Moreno to know what I'm doing."

She pulled out her cell phone and sent a text to the officer waiting up the street in the unmarked car. "Let's go. We'll get lunch before we come back."

Alison parked in front of the garage door and they went inside the house. The house was still a mess. Very little had been put back in place. "Do you know something I don't know?" she asked.

"Just a feeling. I'm betting Moreno's boys come back. Fire. Strafing. I don't expect to come out of this with my house intact."

"Is that why nothing has been done to clean up the mess?"

"Yeah. Why bother?" His expression was grim.

"Let's get started then. Do you have boxes in the garage?"

He limped over to the door into the garage and opened it. And smiled. "In that corner." He pointed.

"Sidney was here already. The SUV is gone." She brought in three boxes to start with and set them in the living room.

Doug looked bemused. "They destroyed my music. I'll miss that. But what I would miss most is my books. Particularly the ones on psychology and the criminal mind." He glanced down at the pile of smashed DVDS. "My favorite movies are gone."

She picked up a box. "Which books do I start with?"

"That top shelf." He pointed to the smaller of the bookcases against the wall.

"I'll do these." He put down his cane and pulled several books off the nearest shelf and put them into the a box on the couch.

Alison took the first box out to her car and opened the trunk. The patrolmen in the unmarked car got out and came over to her.

"Is there something I can do to help?"

"Yes, there's going to be a bunch of boxes to bring out. Doug has a lot of books."

The officer laughed. "I believe that. I've known Doug a long time."

After about thirty minutes, Doug looked around. "That's it for the living room. The rest is for the fire or whatever. Thanks for your help, Jim."

"Glad I was here." He went back outside.

Doug frowned. "No need looking in the kitchen. They even took their crowbars to the skillets. And I got all the clothes that were left whole the last time I was here."

"You'll be doing some shopping when all this is over."

"But there is one more item in the bedroom." His eyes lit up.

She followed him into the bedroom. He reached into the corner of the closet and pulled out a mahogany cane with a carved eagle head.

"That's beautiful. Why don't you use it?"

"This one is good enough." He leaned on his silver-topped cane with fancy scroll work. "I don't deserve the eagle head."

"Why not?"

"I'm not like Apache Joe."

Doug had his secrets too. "What do you mean?"

"I'll explain it someday. If I consider myself ready to use the cane." He handed it to her and she took it.

She examined the intricate carving of the eagle head. "I'll hold you to that. I'm intrigued."

"Let's go." He limped to the living room then turned.

She followed him, carrying the cane.

"Thanks for your help." Doug's eyes held a message. Different from when he gave her that hug earlier.

The vibes between them jumped like electricity, only tamer. Gentler. Yet it scared her on one level. The level that said men used women.

Doug set the silver-headed cane on the couch. She added the eagle-headed cane. He moved closer, waited for her to move too. She did. Like a cord pulled her in his direction. He braced his feet and pulled her into his arms. She couldn't have stopped him now for anything. She wanted his kiss.

When his lips captured hers, he was gentle, probing, and filled her with hope. He deepened the kiss, drawing her in, tantalizing her in a way she'd never felt before. Never had a man treated her so gently, so lovingly.

No need to panic.

When he released her, the sweet smile on his rugged face made everything all right. She was okay with his kiss this time. Could she be healing? Was Doug the one man she could trust completely?

CHAPTER 11

"I'm going to drive down the street next to the agency." Alison glanced at him quickly, then turned back to her driving. "Point out your car to me, so I'll know where it is."

"Okay."

She turned onto the tree-lined side street and headed toward the agency.

"It's the tan Subaru under the oak tree, three houses up."

"I see it. Now I know where to run if you head that way." She smiled and he knew it was genuine, that she trusted him. That she saw the value of having the car parked close by.

She pulled into the agency parking lot and into Doug's space by the door. He was beginning to count on her too much. Was that good? And that kiss. So deep. So tender. Where would it lead? Where did he want it to lead? He had no answer.

Once inside, he headed straight for his office. Rafe was waiting. Sitting in front of the desk. Studying Rafe's face, he couldn't tell if it was good news or bad. "What's up?" He sat behind the desk.

"Our house was tossed this morning while we were all out." A neutral tone, as if he expected it.

"He's letting us know he can find us. Any of us. He's letting us know we're all vulnerable. You could send Sabrina and Gracie out of town."

"I'd rather they came to Jake's with the rest of us."

"That might work. They need protection too."

"Besides, Sabrina's already involved. She and two of her friends went shopping this morning and bought the towels and sheets and kitchen stuff that the house needed."

"Very good." He was surprised at times how generous and capable his staff was. And how their families rallied around too. "Who paid for the stuff?"

"Jake supplied a credit card. Sabrina is on her way to the house now, to unload her van around back, out of sight of the street."

The DEA, still in control. Alarm bells went off inside him. "We need to be extra vigilant. Keep the house a secret for as long as we can. While we wait for someone to locate Moreno's hideout."

"Is Alison bringing you to the house?"

"At the end of the work day. At least that's the plan for now. Unless something changes."

"I can take you if she's needed with Dani."

"Okay. Dani is the highest priority right now. I want to get her moved in soon."

"I can do that too if I need to. Let me know." He stood. "I have errands to run for Jake. See you later." Rafe left and the side door closed.

Doug picked up his cell phone and called Dani. He wanted to hear her voice.

"Dad. Dave is making us hide in the basement."

"Smart thinking on his part. You know your grandmother's house was firebombed in the middle of the night?"

"That's what Dave said. He said we have to hide until time to move." He'd have to remember to thank Dave for thinking of that.

"Where are we going? Will you be there?"

"Yes, before the end of the afternoon. We're going to move into a big house on east Burnside." He leaned back. Loving the sound of his daughter's voice. So many years. "Is there an outside entrance to the basement?"

"Yes."

"Then you're safe. If you hear the smoke alarm upstairs, you know it's a fire and you need to get out."

"He explained all that." Exasperation in her voice.

"We'll be together at Jake's house in a few more hours. You can make it till then."

"Okay, Dad. It's just like I'm scared, really scared."

"I know honey. You have reason to be scared. We all are. We don't know what Moreno's men will do next."

"Okay. I'll stay hidden and see you later."

"Take care. I love you." He ended the call.

Doug stood, intending to check on Erik's progress with the databases, looking at the Mexican nationals in the area, looking for family ties to Moreno.

His cell phone rang. It was Jake. He sat down again. Pain shot up his legs. He'd been on his feet too much lately. The pain rarely went away. He answered the call.

"The DEA task force is meeting at a downtown office building in thirty minutes. Can you make it?"

"What's up?"

"Hensley wants to meet you, since you're the one who's drawing Moreno to Oregon."

"Not my choice that Moreno comes here."

"Oh, they're not blaming you."

He wasn't so sure about that. A major dealer moving into the area was cause for concern in any drug agency. "Sure. I'll come. Alison is here to drive me. Should she come too?"

"Sure. She might as well know who the DEA agents are too." Jake gave him the address and Doug wrote it down. "Second floor conference room, near the elevator."

"We're on our way." He ended the call. He wasn't sure he wanted to get involved with the DEA. That's not what his agency was all about. But the drug trafficking and violence were coming to him. Damn that bastard, Moreno.

DOUG LIMPED SLOWLY DOWN the hallway and stopped outside the door of the second floor conference room, and leaned on his cane. Shadowy figures were visible through the frosted glass. The knot in his gut tightened until it was rock hard. His entire body tensed.

Alison reached for the door knob. "You don't think they're going to offer you the kind of help you need, do you?"

"No. But I have a suspicion of what they want." She pushed open the door and he limped in and closed the door behind them.

Five suits sat at the long wooden table, along with Jake, Nick, and Chet. The DEA contingent consisted of four men and one woman, and were grouped at one end of the table. One man at the end. Hensley, most likely.

He shuffled some papers in front of him. "Come in. Sit down. We were waiting for you." Abrupt words. Not welcoming at all. So that's how it was going to be.

The paper shuffler spoke first. "I'm Special Agent Sean Hensley, leader of this task force. We've been in existence for over a year. We work out of the regional office. To my left are Bob and Will. To my right are Cindy and Jason."

No last names. This wasn't going to be an ongoing relationship.

Hensley cleared his throat. "Our goal here in the Portland area and the Willamette Valley is to contain or disrupt the drug trafficking. Moreno is a key player and his ties to Mexican cartels are well documented." His gaze was directed at Doug.

"Are you going to find Moreno and arrest him quickly, before he kills anyone else?" Doug stared back at him. "His intention is murder."

"That's not what this task force was formed to do. Our job is building a case against Moreno and his gang, and any other drug gangs in the area, that will stand up in court. Capturing him now would be premature."

"You're going to let him kill me? Then you'll arrest him for murder?" No use talking around the subject.

"That's not what I said." Hensley's words were heated.

"My younger daughter was killed last Thursday. My mother's house was firebombed early this morning. She got out alive, thank God. We're all targets. My family and my agency staff." Anger rode the edge of his words.

Hensley flinched. "I'm sorry. But that doesn't change my assignment as head of this task force."

"So why was I summoned to this sham meeting?"

"So we could see who it is that is big enough to bring Moreno out of hiding down in Los Angeles."

At least he was honest. He'd undoubtedly heard Moreno was chasing a cripple. "You do realize, don't you, that part of his goal is to take over the drug trade in the Northwest?"

"That's why documenting his operation is a key objective of this task force."

"Well, stop him now. Surely you have enough documentation to keep him in prison for a long time."

"The cartels have smart lawyers working for them." Hensley's tone indicated frustration. "So does Moreno. We have to make sure we have enough evidence to indict and convict."

"How long is that going to take?" Doug glared at Hensley, then at Chet and Nick in turn. Neither one would meet his gaze. "Do you know where Moreno's hideout is?" He snapped out the accusation.

"No." Hensley lifted his chin. "But we'll find him. And when it comes time to arrest him, we'll be coordinating the SWAT teams and local police presence. To take him alive."

"Before that happens, he'll do a lot more damage." They were on their own. Except for the police help supplied by Chet and Nick and the unmarked cars. And Jake was reporting back to Hensley, since he was a part of the task force.

"That can't be helped. It's not this particular task force's job to protect you and your people."

"If he's shooting at me, I'll shoot back." Doug laced his words with anger. "We may both die. But I'd like to live to get to know my surviving daughter."

Hensley stood and stared down at Doug. "You won't be in on the take down. You stay out of it. The task force has the job of grabbing Moreno."

"He won't let me stay out of it. He's the one coming after me." This meeting was all about keeping him from going after Moreno himself. Inside Doug seethed. That rock hard lump in his gut screamed at him. Alison reached over and patted his leg under the table. He glanced at her, at the compassion in her eyes.

"Stay safe. Stay out of the way." Hensley picked up his papers, a signal the meeting was over.

Message delivered. Hensley believed Doug was the problem.

CHAPTER 12

*A*lison dropped Doug at the office, then drove to her apartment, to pick up more clothes and other items she'd need at Jake's safe house. She took the stairs to the second floor, instead of the rickety elevator.

Halfway down the hall, she stopped. Her heart sped up, pounding in her chest. A knot formed in her stomach. Her door stood open. So much for building security. She pulled her gun from her shoulder holster, took off the safety, and checked for a bullet in the chamber.

No sounds came from her apartment. She leaned against the wall, staying where she was, slowing her breathing, listening, waiting.

After a good ten minutes of waiting, she crept forward, gun gripped in her hands. She stepped through the door, watching for movement. Nothing.

Except a total mess. The knot in her stomach tightened. Her apartment had been literally torn apart, like Doug's house.

The landlord would not be happy about the damaged furniture. But the building security hadn't kept the gang members out.

She checked the bedroom, bathroom, and kitchen. No one hiding. Just the mess. Her remaining suitcase was slashed and destroyed. She found several grocery sacks in the kitchen and stuffed in the clothes that were salvageable. Her favorite sweater had been ripped in several places. Luckily she'd already taken most of her best clothes with her when she went to Dave's. She hadn't had a huge wardrobe to begin with. Very few items of any value. Her life had to be portable. She'd been living with the threat of Kenny finding her since the prison gates had closed behind him.

Her cell phone rang. It was Kara. She answered.

"Alison, could you relieve me at Dave's for a while? My roommate is in hysterics. Our apartment was tossed today, and everything is a total wreck."

"I'm at my apartment. Same thing here."

"Oh, no. What will you do?"

"Clean it up after Moreno is no longer a threat."

"It could get worse," Kara said. "His boys could start shooting."

"I'm sure we'll see that before this is over. I'm almost finished picking out what clothes are still wearable. I'll come to Dave's as soon as I can. Tell Dani to pack her stuff and be ready to go."

"I will. Thanks. Angela is freaking out. I need to go calm her down and get what clothes I can for myself."

"Is there somewhere Angela can go, since you'll be at Jake's?"

"I'll talk to her about that when I get there."

"See you in a few." She ended the call and took another look around. Then picked up the two shopping bags she'd filled and locked the door behind her. Then laughed. Lot of good locking a door does with Moreno's gang around.

She started the engine of the Taurus, turned on the air conditioner, then called Doug and let him know what happened.

"I was going to call you," he said. "Where are you?"

"Getting ready to leave my apartment. I'm in the car. Things are happening fast."

"Tell me about it. Chet just told me my house was fire-bombed and it's a total loss."

"Oh, no. At least Kara and I weren't firebombed, but our apartments were tossed, like your house was on Saturday."

"Thanks for helping me get my stuff out of the house. Anything can happen."

"You need to get to Jake's now. Not wait till later." She kept her words as calm as she could.

"Where are you heading?"

"Kara called me in a panic. Her roommate got home, saw the mess, and freaked out. I'm going to relieve her at Dave's so she can deal with Angela and the police. I didn't bother the police about mine."

"Erik and I are the only ones in the office now. I'll call Rafe and see if he can pick me up from somewhere that Erik can take me. Rafe is using Sabrina's van to go in and out at Jake's."

"Good thinking. Once you're safely there, call me and I'll bring Dani. I assume Dave will ride his bike. Let me know if there's any problems."

"I will. You be careful." He ended the call.

She paused. Her responsibility was to get Doug's surviving daughter into the house safely. She couldn't fail.

ALISON PARKED behind Dave's house, in the gravel next to the garage. And called his cell phone. He answered.

"I'm outside in the back. Are you still in the basement?"

"Yes. Kara will let you in the back door, then she's leaving. Come on down to our cramped quarters."

"We should get word shortly to make the move to Jake's."

"I'm staying here. We need someone on the outside."

"We'll talk about it." She ended the call and got out of her car and locked it.

Kara stood at the back door, holding it open. "I'm sorry. I panicked. I should have told Angela to call the police and handle it herself."

Alison passed by her. "That's okay, we need to keep on the move. And you need clothes too. Salvage what you can. Doug's house was firebombed and destroyed. He's heading for Jake's."

The expression on Kara's face registered up there close to terror. "I'm scared."

"Go calm Angela down, then go to Jake's, but watch for a tail and watch for the unmarked police cars."

"Okay. See you later." Kara headed to her car parked in front of the garage.

Alison locked the back door, then opened the door down to the basement, and descended the wooden stairs. And was hit by the musty smell of a damp basement. Dani was perched on a bean bag chair, next to a pile of boxes. A small TV sat on another big box, blaring out some talk show. Dave was sitting on a folding chair, amid more boxes and piled furniture. Neither looked happy.

Their greetings were strained. No one knew what would happen next. It was like waiting for that proverbial last shoe to fall.

"Has Doug called you?" She directed her question at Dave.

"No."

"His house was firebombed."

"No." Dani jumped up. "Are these people like insane?"

"Ruthless, violent, crafty. That's how I'd describe them." Alison glanced around for a place to sit.

She settled for an overstuffed chair that sank down to the springs when she sat on it. She turned to Dani. "Once your father is in the house, we'll get the call to go."

"Good. I want out of this dungeon." Dani flipped the channel on the small TV to the late afternoon news. And saw her father's house in flames. "I can't watch this." She turned the channel back to the talk show she'd been watching.

"Now, what's this about you wanting to stay here by yourself?" Alison focused her gaze on Dave. "Don't you want the power of numbers to be in your favor?"

"What if you all go up in flames tonight. Someone has to be around to identify you."

"I don't like your humor."

"And I don't…"

The rat-tat-tat of automatic gunfire penetrated the basement. Alison jumped up, her heart in her throat. She grabbed Dani and shoved her over to the front wall of the basement, as close as they could get, then hung onto her. "Get over here, Dave." The barrage of bullets went on and on. One burst after another.

"What's going on?" Dani's voice was panicked.

"Automatic rifle fire." Dave joined them next to the shelving unit piled with junk. "I've heard that sound before." He picked up his phone. "We have an emergency. Gunshots outside my house." He gave the dispatcher the address and disconnected.

"We could have been up there." Now Dani's voice was shaky.

Alison expected tears at any time. "That's right." She tried to keep her voice steady, not let Dani know how terrified she was.

"There goes my big screen TV. Those bullets are putting holes in everything."

"Will they come down here?" Panic again in Dani's voice.

"No. They're firing out of a car and hitting the house with as much as they can in a short time. Then they'll leave." Dave's tone was grim.

Alison strained to hear. "There's been at least fifty shots. They're hanging around a long time." She had a terrifying thought. Would someone come barging down those stairs? She let go of Dani and pulled out her gun. And trained it on the stairway.

"Why are you doing that?" Dani shrunk away from her.

"Because I don't take chances. These guys are unpredictable."

The shots stopped, the silence almost worse than the noise. Now what? Alison moved close to the stairs, at the side. Close to where someone would come down. Close to where she could get a good shot.

Then they heard sirens. Several of them. The police had arrived. The shooters were long gone.

Relief flooded through her. Her phone rang. She pulled it from her pocket and answered. It was Chet.

"Where are you guys? Are you all right?" His voice was unsteady.

"We're in the basement. We're okay. Are you outside?"

"I'm on my way. Four patrol cars answered the 911 call. I assume Dave made the call."

"Yes, he did."

"The guys outside will be relieved they won't encounter dead bodies, riddled with bullets."

"Should we come up, or let them come to us?"

"It's safe now. Go out the front door, where the officers are." He ended the call.

"Let's go." She holstered her gun.

Dani grabbed her backpack that was on the floor by the bean bag chair. Alison picked up her suitcase. At the top of the stairs, Dave opened the door carefully, making sure no one was on the other side.

"Oh, what a mess." Dave stared at his living room, at his shattered TV. At the holes in the walls and furniture. "That security system didn't help at all."

"We could have been sitting there." Dani's voice still held panic.

Alison put her arm around Dani and led her to what was left of the front door. "That's why Dave made you go to the basement. He was afraid something like this might happen."

"I didn't think it could be this bad."

"We're all finding out how violent these men are. Remember, they killed your sister, they burned your grandmother's house, they burned your dad's house."

Once outside Dani seemed bewildered by all the people standing around. "I hope they catch all of them."

The officers put up crime scene tape. Chet arrived, followed closely by Nick.

"The two patrol cars in pursuit stopped the vehicle and they were fired on," Nick said. "They fired back. Two officers were shot, the two gunmen were shot and killed. The driver is in custody."

Alison set down Dani's suitcase and looked back at the house." I guess you're going to have to come to Jake's after all."

Dave winced. "I sure can't stay here tonight. I have a Swiss cheese house now."

"You're never serious, are you?" Dani shouted at him. "You keep making jokes out of everything."

"It's either that or go crazy."

"Now might be a good time to slip away and go to Jake's." Alison picked up the suitcase again. "My car is around back."

"I have a bag packed and in the garage," Dave said. "Just in case. I'll put it in your car, and I'll ride my bike. I don't want to leave it here."

Chet approached them. "Has anyone called Doug yet?"

"We didn't." Alison gasped. "Too much going on."

"I'll let him know what happened. You guys get going. Your escorts are down the street. I'll alert them that you're leaving through the alley, out the back."

"Thanks, Chet." Dave led the way around the side of the house, Dani followed, then Alison.

So far she was hanging together. Later tonight, when she was alone, she knew the reality would hit her. They came so close to being killed.

CHAPTER 13

*E*ven with the police cars behind them, Alison's nerves were stretched almost beyond capacity. She gripped the steering wheel, her knuckles white. What if Jake's house had already been spotted as belonging to the agency group? What if they were still targets tonight? Another car, more shooters? Far more questions than answers.

Dani rode in silence, crouched down in the seat, like she was trying to be as invisible as possible.

"Are we almost there?" Dani's question was almost a whisper.

"Little bit further. Five minutes maybe."

Alison drove cautiously, watching for anything out of the ordinary, even though she knew she had an escort. When she got to the section of East Burnside where the house was located, she slowed, so she wouldn't miss the driveway tucked behind the hedge on the right hand side of the property. She'd found the house online and knew what it looked like. Pale green, pointed roof, lots of trees and shrubs. An older house with a wide driveway that curved around behind the house, so she'd be parking out of sight of the street.

Dave kept his motorcycle about a half block behind her. Extra surveillance. She found the house without a problem and pulled into the driveway and around to the back. Dave followed. Only then did she relax her grip on the steering wheel. They'd made it this far. Now what?

The back door opened and Doug limped down the few steps from the porch. Dani flung the car door open and ran to her dad, throwing herself into his arms. Sobbing and hiccupping and clinging to him.

"Oh, baby. I'm sorry this is all happening. It's my fault." Doug cradled her in his arms. "I never should have tried so hard to run Moreno out of Los Angeles."

"He's a rotten SOB." Jake waited by the open door. "You slowed him down. We'll get him this time."

Alison opened her trunk. "I want this to end, before someone else gets killed." She grabbed her bags and Jake moved off the porch to let her pass.

Dani and Dave took their own bags and they went inside, through the large kitchen to the dining room. Rafe and Sabrina were in the living room on the couch, watching the early newscast covering the shooting at Dave's house.

Alison greeted them then stared at the TV screen. Icy cold waves of piercing nerves cascaded down her spine. All those bullet holes. And they had been inside, in the basement. The sound of that rifle fire would haunt her for a long time.

The reporter was saying there was no word on injuries or deaths. The police hadn't released a statement. "Are the facts being withheld from the media?" Her question was not directed at a specific person.

"For now." Doug had come up behind her. "They're not

letting Moreno know if he's scored any hits. They did announce that the gunmen were apprehended, that they were shot and killed when they fired on the officers."

"Hooray for our side," Dave said.

Doug reached out and gripped Alison's arm. "Thank you, for all you've done for Dani, for keeping her safe." His eyes were moist.

"It wasn't all me. Dave gets most of the credit. Thinking about using that cramped basement saved our lives." He let his hand drop, but the message in his eyes showed that he cared and that he appreciated her.

She turned away. Not something to think about now. "Are we all here?"

"Kara is still with her roommate, but she'll be here shortly," Doug said. "Scott and Erik are stopping for some supplies on their way."

"I'll take you upstairs and show you where you'll be sleeping." Jake led them up the stairs.

Doug followed, slowly dragging his right leg up each step. Alison understood his need to stay close to Dani. But his pain was evident in his eyes and in the set of his jaw.

Jake pointed out the bedrooms and the bed assignments. All but one of the bedrooms was large enough to hold more than one bed, and enough beds had been delivered that morning. Everyone would be sleeping comfortably.

Alison would share a room with Dani. Kara had the small room. Rafe and Sabrina would share a room with their daughter, Gracie. Doug and Jake were in another room. Dave, Erik, and Scott in the last one. Ten people living in one big house. There were two bathrooms upstairs and she'd seen one half bath by the back door when they'd come in. She only hoped

Moreno would be caught soon and they wouldn't have to stay long.

Jake opened up a small closet-like room on the back of the house, that also had a window. "Here's our backyard guard tower." He laughed, but it sounded hollow. "I'll bring in a chair and small table."

"I'll take first watch in the front." Dave went into the room he'd be sharing with Erik and Scott and pulled a chair over to the window.

Alison and Dani put away their clothes while Doug watched from the doorway. It made her self-conscious, but she understood that he didn't want to let Dani out of his sight for now.

When she'd finished, she went to the door. "I don't feel safe here." She kept her voice low. "A firebomb would be a complete disaster."

"Scott's working on a solution. More rope ladders, a sling to get me down quickly." He blushed, if you could call it that. He knew he was mocking his disability. He often did, to keep himself in perspective.

"And one more thing," he said. "At least two people will be on watch at all times. One upstairs in the front and one in the back. Scott's also bringing extra fire extinguishers."

"I didn't think we would all sleep at the same time."

"Oh, no. We're under siege here. It's wartime tactics until this is over. We'll survive. And we'll get Moreno."

"I'm glad you're so positive. I can't share your optimism. Frankly, I'm terrified."

"Looks to me like you're holding up fine. Consider what you've done so far today. You and Dave saved Dani."

She only hoped Moreno didn't find out about this house. Far too many targets in one place. She didn't like the survival odds. And the odds plummeted with each attack.

THE EXTRA VOICES downstairs alerted Doug that the others had arrived. He grasped the top of the banister and carefully maneuvered down the stairs, using his cane for balance. He didn't want to embarrass himself in front of his daughter.

Dani followed him down, then smiled shyly at him.

He stopped at the bottom of the stairs. "I can still get around." Another shy smile.

"Doug. Dinnertime." Rafe's voice came from the dining room.

He ignored Rafe. His whole focus was on Dani.

She looked up at him. "I'm remembering things now. Like how you held me on your lap and like read stories to me. You haven't changed a whole lot."

He laughed. "You have. You were four when you left. Losing my darling little girls left me heartbroken."

Her eyes filled with unshed tears. "I want to get to know you, now that I've found you." She pushed her long brown hair back from her face. "And I want to get to know my grand-mother. I don't want to die. I don't want you to die. Or her. I haven't even met her yet."

"And I'll do everything I possibly can to keep all of us alive. Every single one of us."

"Dinner." Rafe's voice was insistent.

"Coming." He put his left arm around Dani and walked her into the dining room. "Rafe is our self-appointed chef. He loves to cook and to feed people."

Doug glanced at the array of food. "He didn't have time to cook today."

Rafe and Sabrina had used a long, narrow table to assemble a buffet of ham, roast chicken, and salads, all brought from a deli. With breads and condiments to go with the main dishes. Glasses of water and iced tea sat along the middle of the dining room table.

Sabrina set the stack of heavy paper plates at one end of the buffet and smiled at Doug. She had come out of her shell. And changed her wardrobe. No more hiding behind bulky clothes. She wore jeans and a light sweater and looked radiant. She and Rafe were good for each other. Doug was secretly pleased he had looked the other way when they had fallen in love.

"No need to wait for me." Doug set his cane against the wall and picked up a plate. "But I'm not bashful. I'll start at the head of the line." He limped to the buffet and filled his plate, then sat at the table.

Dani was right behind him. At least the trauma of the day hadn't affected her appetite.

Erik went upstairs to get Dave. As soon as everyone had filled their plates and sat down, Doug tapped his fork against his water glass.

"This is the only meal we'll all sit down and eat together. We're going to have to be on high alert. At least two people on watch at all times, one in front and one in the back."

"Surely they haven't found us this quickly." Scott grabbed a glass of iced tea and set it by his plate.

Doug gazed around the table at all the people he cared about. "First, an apology. I'm sorry my feud with Moreno has caused so many problems for everyone."

"We'll get through this," Rafe said. "Moreno is frustrated because he can't find Dani."

"And he's not going to." Anger laced Doug's words.

Alison sat across the table from him, intent on eating. She'd been kept too busy. He hoped she was getting enough food and sleep.

She jumped when her cell phone rang. She pulled it out of her pocket. "I'm sorry. It's...someone important. I need to take this call." She got up and went into the living room.

He could hear snippets of her side of the conversation. Alison was upset and not trying to hide it. She finished the call and returned to the table, her expression tense.

"A problem? Can we help?"

"I don't know." She sat down again. "It was my last foster mother. Sophie Kendrick."

"Is she okay?" Doug asked. "You're upset."

"She's okay, but someone broke into her house while she was shopping this afternoon. Whoever it was stole money and jewelry, then took her address book off the dining room table."

"Her address book?" Doug's suspicious mind took over. "Where does she live?"

"In central California, in a town called Exeter. She moved there shortly after I graduated from high school. I've visited her several times, the last time on my way back to Oregon last spring."

By then everyone had stopped eating and were listening intently. "If you don't want to talk about it now, we can wait until later."

"This concerns all of us, since I'm staying." She glanced around the table. "Kenny Driscoll, my ex-husband, knew about Sophie. Kenny was supposed to get out of San Quentin any day now. He must have been released. If he is the one who broke in and has the address book, he knows where I live and the location of the agency."

"And what is Kenny after?" Rafe asked.

"He wants to kill me." She raised her chin. "He told me he'd come after me when he got out of prison and slice me up with his switchblade." She stared straight at Rafe when she said it.

Doug ached for her. He knew how hard it was for her to open up and say something like that.

"If it's him," Rafe said, "he's breaking his parole by coming to Oregon. He's from L.A., right?"

Doug nodded. "And I told Alison she needs to stay here where there are other people who can help her." He glanced around the table. "If anyone has an objection, speak up now."

"She can't leave," Kara said. "He'd find her and she wouldn't have help. We can help."

"Of course we can," Rafe said.

"One other thing to consider," Jake said. "Is this going to be a distraction that could put this house in jeopardy, with all its occupants?"

"Is that the DEA perspective?" Doug asked.

"Yes, it's the DEA perspective. The task force has spent time and money building a case against Moreno's gang and its affiliates. We need this operation to go down as planned."

"As planned by whom?" Doug was beginning to regret allowing a DEA agent into the agency. "Are Moreno and his gang calling the shots?"

"Of course not," Jake said. "Okay. I understand. I'm helping the agency. We're in this together." His words carried a tone of insincerity.

"So we have three people in this house who are in real danger," Scott said. "Dani, Doug, and Alison."

Doug shook his head. "Alison is targeted by Moreno as well as her ex. Moreno knew who she was when she was down in Los Angeles last year."

Erik put an outraged expression on his face. "What are the rest of us? Collateral damage?"

Nervous laughter broke out in the room. Doug pushed aside his plate. "Actually, everyone is in danger. Because you are all connected to me in some way. We have to make sure we're well protected here. And be extremely careful when we leave or arrive."

"You're not mandating we all stay here all the time?" Erik asked.

"Not practical. We need to maintain a presence at the agency. Look like a business. And see if we can figure out a way to spot Moreno's gang members."

"Do we have any information about the driver caught after the shooting?" Erik got up from the table and went back for second helpings on ham and potato salad.

"Nick said he'd call later with an update," Doug said.

Jake stood. "I shouldn't be telling you this, but I think you need to know. The DEA had an agent embedded with Moreno down in Los Angeles. They did not want Moreno to come up to Portland, because they didn't want their agent involved in Moreno's vendetta against Doug."

He went to the buffet table and refilled his ice tea glass, then sat down again.

"More complications," Alison said.

Doug looked around. "That does put a different spin on things. I thought the DEA wanted him up here so they could take him, away from his usual haunts."

"The DEA wants this feud with you to go away," Jake said. "But they don't have any idea how to get that to happen. They're in the middle of an immense evidence gathering phase and don't want it interrupted or sabotaged."

"Yet your position at the agency gives us a direct link to the task force."

"Window dressing," Jake said. "That way they can keep tabs on you and what communications you get from Moreno or someone in his gang."

"What about Chet and Nick?" Doug's gut clenched, as he waited for Jake's answer.

"The DEA wants to know what the local cops are doing too." Jake's tone indicated it was business as usual.

"So we wait here like sitting ducks until something happens," Alison said. "Hiding, when we know the problem won't go away. None of the problems."

"We also have to keep the business running," Doug said. "While we keep this place a complete secret. That's our number one priority."

CHAPTER 14

One teenager. One young adult. Both afraid. Both lonely in a house full of people. Alison resisted calling out to Gracie when she scooted up the stairs as soon as dinner was over. What would she say to her? That she understood? That she'd been in the foster care system herself? That Gracie was lucky to be back with her mother.

But was she? The entire agency was under siege. At least it felt like it.

Then there was Dani. She'd come all the way from Florida so her father could protect her. And she'd been in that basement when the shooting started. Of course she was scared. She hid in front of the television, distracting herself by watching whatever was on.

Why couldn't one teenager and one young adult comfort each other? Worth a try.

Alison found Dani in front of the television, as she'd expected. "Hey, come into the den with me for a minute, will you?"

"Sure." Dani gave her a questioning look, but followed her down the hall to the den. Two computers had been set up, but no one was in there working. Dani plopped onto a chair.

Alison sat on the couch. "Have you and Gracie had a chance to talk yet?"

"No. She went back upstairs. She's like real scared. I heard what she said to her mother."

"They were separated for fourteen years. She's only been with her mother since April, when your father found her in a foster home and arranged to take her to her mother."

"Oh, gee. No wonder she's worried." Her open expression gave Alison hope.

"How about you trying to be a big sister to Gracie while she's here. Could you do that?"

"I can try." Dani frowned. "I lost my sister. It feels strange not having her to talk to. She was only nineteen."

"Yeah. Too young to die. Wait here. I'll find Gracie." Alison left the room and went upstairs to the bedroom Gracie shared with her mother and Rafe.

She knocked on the door. "Gracie, are you in there?"

"Yes." Her voice was muffled.

"Could I talk to you, please? It's Alison."

Gracie opened the door and pushed it back. Alison stayed in the doorway. "Dani is downstairs in the den. She'd like to talk to you. Did you know her younger sister was killed?"

"Rafe told me. I don't want to be here. I don't want to die and I don't want anything to happen to my mother or Rafe." Panic rode her words.

"That's why we're in this big house, all together, so we can protect each other."

"Fire and bullets can still get through."

"You're right. But Dani can tell you how she and Dave and I escaped the rifle fire at his house."

Gracie shifted on her feet, nervous energy emanating from her teenage body.

"Come on downstairs and talk to Dani. I think it will help you. Instead of staying up here all alone with your thoughts."

She hesitated a moment. "Okay." A tentative word.

They walked down the stairs side by side. Then Alison led the way to the den. Dani had moved to the couch.

"Go ahead. Sit down with Dani. I'm sure the two of you can find plenty to talk about. Dani is in college, but only eight years older than you are."

Gracie sat on the couch and tried to smile. It was a bit lopsided, but a good attempt. "Hi, Dani. I'm sorry about your sister."

"Thanks. She shouldn't have had to die." Dani shifted so she was facing Gracie.

"No one should have to die." Gracie also turned toward Dani.

Alison silently left the room and returned to the living room. The girls would bond. Both were trying. She sat next to Sabrina on the big sectional sofa. "I just took Gracie into the den to talk to Dani. I hope you don't mind. I didn't think she ought to be by herself."

"Oh, that's good. I didn't know what to tell her to do. She's afraid, but we can't go back to the house and stay by ourselves."

"No, you can't. Too dangerous. We'll make this situation work here."

Doug limped over to them and sat on the sofa. "Where's Dani? I saw her leave with you."

"I put Dani and Gracie in the den so they could get to know

one another." She gazed at him. "I thought Dani could be a big sister to Gracie and help her cope. Is that okay?"

"More than okay. Brilliant. I was wondering what to do for Dani. Big sister to Gracie sounds like a great solution."

Jake approached where they were sitting. He'd been watching from across the room. Alison was not sure how this was going to work out, with Jake as a member of the DEA and the renter of this so-called safe house.

"Doug, let's go to the dining room where we can talk." Jake gestured in that direction.

"Okay." Doug grabbed his cane and left the room with him.

DOUG SAT at the end of the dining room table, next to the window that offered a view of the back yard and parking area. He stretched out his throbbing right leg. Jake had a scowl on his face. A tight knot formed in Doug's gut.

"I didn't think this setup would work." Jake sat to his left. "Now I know it won't. How are you going to get everyone out in the morning to go work at the agency?"

"We'll be driving around the city the same as we have been, with our police escorts."

"And I'll be staying here? Since I don't have a role at the agency?"

"You'll continue your DEA business with Hensley." He shifted on the chair, to try for a more comfortable position. "Work here or go where you need to go. It's not business as usual for any of us."

"Okay." Jake wore a troubled expression, knitted brows, his lips set in a grim line.

"Oh, you're wondering if you're going to be expected to watch over the girls. No, that's not your responsibility."

"Good." He shifted on his chair.

That wasn't all he wanted to say, obviously. Doug waited. Anyone else and he would have taken the lead. But Jake was new. Not really agency. Still DEA in job and in heart. A huge conflict of interest because of Moreno's current tactics.

"Who will be here during the day?"

"Dave volunteered, since he doesn't have another agency assignment right now. Sabrina will be here too. Gracie's mother. And Gracie and Dani."

Doug hesitated, then asked his own question. "What are your instructions? What does Hensley expect you to do?"

"Take care of task force business."

"Which is?"

"I'm not at liberty to say. We have our orders to carry out."

"That's what I thought. So, you use your days to carry out task force business. And your nights are spent here with us as part of the group."

"That's the way I see it. I have my work, you have your work. And I'm helping you by providing this safe house."

"Thank you for setting it all up. That was a help."

"You're welcome." Stiff words.

"If you're not comfortable being a part of the group, you can go somewhere else to stay. You don't have to stay here."

"I'll give it a couple of days and see what happens. And check with Hensley. See what he wants me to do."

Doug stared at him hard. He was DEA all the way. "Okay, we'll continue as we are for now. Wait for Moreno's next move."

"He may not do anything but build his drug empire here."

"Then why was my daughter murdered? Why were our houses tossed, my mother's house firebombed, my house completely destroyed? Why was Dave's house strafed by automatic rifles?"

"He wants you to know he's here."

"He called me. I know he's here. How close are you to building a case against him? Weeks? Months? Years?"

"We've only been monitoring him for three years, when we saw how powerful he was getting in Mexico. He's importing drugs for at least two cartels we know of for sure."

"So, you aren't close." A statement, not a question.

"No. We're not close. We need more time. Your feud with him is upsetting him and we're not getting any more information about shipments. He's stopped importing for now, from what we can see."

"So that's what Hensley is so uptight about. No more intelligence gathering to help your case."

"You could say that."

"I just did."

"Moreno has concentrated his resources on you and your agency. He sent that guy to Florida after your daughters."

"And he only got one of them."

"The shooter paid for that mistake with his life. We have confirmation on that."

Doug's heart beat faster. "That's comforting, after the fact. You might have told me sooner." A life for a life.

"Sorry. Wasn't thinking." He stood to leave. Then sat down. "Where do we stand?"

Doug saw some hesitation from Jake. He didn't know himself what he ought to be doing. Interesting.

"Right now, I don't know." Doug hesitated. "I don't know where your loyalties will lie when the firing starts. And it will."

"Here? Or somewhere else?"

Doug narrowed his eyes. "What I want and what my people

want is to locate Moreno. Send in a SWAT team to arrest him for murder and attempted murder."

"You can't do that. That would interfere with the DEA investigation."

"It's my life on the line, and the lives of all my people. Your investigation can go to hell. Tell that to Hensley." Doug stood and stared at Jake. "Does the DEA have any men looking for the hideout?"

Jake grimaced. "We're searching databases for indications of where the house could be."

"It won't be in your databases. He hasn't been here long enough."

"You could be right."

Doug picked up his cane and waved it in the air. "Your first priority is to find out where these guys are coming from who keep attacking my people."

"That's not our job. We're building a case, not doing protection work."

"Come now. DEA agents do all sorts of jobs during an investigation."

"Of course. We're well trained."

"So, use that training to figure out where Moreno is hiding until he's ready to meet me in battle. Because that's what he promised when he called me."

Pain shot down Doug's leg. He dropped back into the chair, trying to get comfortable. "I've known Moreno for years. He's always violent, unpredictable, vengeful." Anger rode the razor-sharp edge of his words.

"Which is why he's after you." Jake's words matched anger with anger. "Why he killed your daughter. Why he's after your other daughter. You two need to leave town so we can take down Moreno our way."

"I don't have years to wait."

"We're building a case."

Doug leaned forward. "Stopping him is more important than building an airtight case for the courtroom."

"He could walk away with the right lawyers." Jake's voice escalated in tone.

"There are indictments against him dating back years. Try him on any number of charges." Anger gnawed at Doug's gut. They were going to end on a stalemate.

"We can't right now."

"Moreno is not running me out of Portland." Doug rose, grabbed his cane again. "If he comes after me, I'll kill him myself."

CHAPTER 15

*D*oug glanced back at the house as Alison pulled out of the driveway. Jake stood at the front window, watching them leave. He'd meant what he told Jake last night. Moreno was not running him out of Portland.

He didn't like giving up driving. He didn't like giving up control. He didn't like giving up his future security to the whims of a madman. Today he'd look into what extra precautions they could make so everyone stayed safe.

When they arrived at the office, Alison parked in the handicapped space, by the door.

Once inside, Doug limped into his office. No computer. No desk chair. Erik had moved them. Okay, no more privacy. They had to keep to the plan. He headed for the conference room. His chair was at the end of the table, in front of his computer. He set down his briefcase. They had been the last to arrive.

He greeted everyone and sat in his chair. "No more private offices for a while. And we don't have the benefit of cubicles to muffle noises. Stay in here as much as you can."

"We can make it work." Rafe handed Doug his favorite mug, full of steaming coffee. "I'll keep your cup full."

"Ah, yes. Priorities. And now I need to call my mother and see how she's doing at her friend's house." He pushed his chair back from the table.

The conversation in the room stopped. He pulled his cell phone from his briefcase and called. The phone kept ringing. She wasn't good at keeping track of her phone. Finally, she answered.

"Doug, are you all right?"

"I'm fine. How are you? Are you over the worst of the scare?"

"I'm worried for you. I saw that shooting on the news last night and I just knew it was someone from your agency." At least she hadn't seen anything about his house being firebombed.

"It was Dave's house on the news. He was in the basement when the shooting happened. The only ones hurt were two policemen and the two shooters. The police killed the shooters." He deliberately left out that Dani was in that basement too.

"You will be careful, won't you? I don't want to lose you too." Sadness leaked through her tone.

"Can you stay there at your friend's and not go anywhere? Please, for now. No lunches, shopping, or going out in public."

"But that guy doesn't know where I am. Maybe he doesn't know what I look like, just where my house is."

"We can't take that chance. Please. Just a few days. Let's see what happens. I have a feeling this isn't going to drag out for long."

"I don't like it. But, okay. I won't go out. We canceled the luncheon. I'll stay inside the house or in the backyard. It has a high fence. But I won't stay here forever."

"You don't have to. I'll keep you updated on what's happening. I wasn't going to tell you yet..." He took a deep breath. "But...my house was firebombed yesterday and completely destroyed."

"Oh, dear. You weren't there, were you?"

"No. I was here at the office. I want you to stay safe. Stay where you are. I'll keep in touch. I love you." He ended the call.

"Do you think she's scared enough to stay hidden?" Alison was leaning against the table.

"I hope so. At least that party got canceled. That had me worried."

A phone rang on the table and Kara picked it up. Rafe and Erik resumed their conversation, keeping their voices down.

Kara ended her call, then Rafe stood. "If they were going to fire on this building, where would they start? At the front, or the side street?"

"Okay, let's talk about this." Doug pushed his chair away from his computer so he could see their faces. "Would they want to hit all four sides? The bricks are on the front and along the parking lot. The back and side street don't have bricks."

"If I were the shooters," Scott said, "I'd start along the front, taking out the windows and the door. Then I'd drive into the lot and get the side door and any cars there. Head out around the back and come down the side street, taking out all the windows on that side. Then I'd take off down the street. One quick pass around the whole building."

"That would take a minute or so," Alison said. "When they hit Dave's house, they slowed and concentrated all the fire power on the front of the house. Then took off at high speed."

Doug drained his coffee cup and set it down. "They don't know where we are in the building. Would they risk the parking lot side and the back? They could get trapped. I'd say the street side and then the front. Even with the brick facing, a lot of shots could go through the door and the windows."

"Or they could reverse and do the front, then the side street." Rafe brought the coffee pot over and filled Doug's cup. "Luckily the restrooms and break room are on the parking lot side, behind bricks."

"But we don't want to spend any more time out of this room than we have to." Doug used his commander in chief tone. "Staying safe is our highest priority. Alison found that out at Dave's." He wanted to hug Dave for thinking of using the basement. Three lives saved yesterday. Losing Dani too would have about killed him. He glanced at Alison. His feelings for her were growing by the day. He couldn't lose her now.

Doug tried to keep a stoic look on his face, regretting his decision for business as usual. "We don't have to stay here. We can go back to Jake's."

"We're here. We might as well stay." Alison retrieved a box of donuts from the table at the side and passed them around.

"Now, after all of that, is there any way we can get any work done?" Doug laughed at himself. "I started something."

"It needed to be said." Kara scooted back from the table. "I'll go grab a few more things from the break room." She went out the door and closed it behind her.

Doug turned on his computer. "And now I'm going to try to forget all of this and check the websites I need to look at." And listen for the sound of gunfire.

ALISON'S personal cell phone in her pocket vibrated. She set down the summary of Kara's insurance case that she'd been reading for her. She pulled out the phone. Her lawyer again.

Everyone in the room was concentrating on work, but she'd have to take the call in here. Couldn't risk going out into the hall.

"Sorry to interrupt. I have to take this call." Tension gripped her entire body. She answered.

"I'm afraid I don't have good news, Alison," William Hughes said. He'd been her lawyer since all the troubles with Kenny had started.

"He's out? And missing?" The tension increased.

"You guessed right."

"Someone broke into my foster mother's house in Exeter yesterday and stole money, jewelry, and her address book." She tried to keep the tremor out of her voice.

"He never reported to his parole officer in Los Angeles yesterday, as he'd been instructed to do."

"Because he was far away already."

"Will he be able to find you with that address book?"

"I'm not using my apartment right now, but I am still working and the agency numbers are in there." She glanced up. Everyone in the room was watching her. All activity had stopped.

"Are you all alone, or is there someone who can help you?" Pure compassion in his voice. That was comforting.

"I have people here with me who can help. And I'm armed myself."

"You shot him once. Do you think you could do it again if you had to?"

"I'd hit him in a vital spot the next time. My shooting skills have improved."

"I don't normally condone violence, but in Kenny's case, I'd say it's warranted if he tries to harm you."

"He intends to slice me up with his switchblade. Remember,

that's what he told me in the courtroom." Doug had moved close to her. He put his hand on her arm. A touch for support. Tears formed behind her eyes.

"I do remember him saying that."

"I have enough scars. He's not going to get to me again. I'll stop him any way I can." She glanced at Kara, at the sheen of tears in her eyes. What was her history?

"Just be careful. I'll let his parole officer know where he's headed. A parole violation warrant will be issued for his arrest."

"I hope they catch him before he gets here."

"I'll keep you informed when I hear anything. Watch out for him."

"Oh, I will. Thank you." She ended the call then sat there with the phone in her hand. Confirmed. Had to have been Kenny at Sophie's yesterday. He could get to Portland at any time. Kara stood and hugged her. Maybe she'd been wrong, keeping her secrets.

"He's not getting close to you." Menace rode Doug's words. He limped back to the table space he was using and made a call.

Alison couldn't tell who he was talking to, but he was asking about the mug shot of Kenny. He ended the call.

"Nick is bringing over a mug shot. We all need to know what this guy looks like. Before he gets here."

"That's good." Rafe stood and reached for some folders in the middle of the table.

"And he said there's two unmarked cars outside watching the place. SERT is on alert. We're high priority now."

Alison leaned back. Maybe, just maybe, Kenny would be caught by an officer assigned to protect them from Moreno. She envisioned him pinned down in the cross fire. She picked up the insurance summary again.

The first shot shattered the window on the front door.

CHAPTER 16

"On the floor." Doug's shout was instinctive. He dropped down, letting his left leg take the brunt of the contact. Pain shot up his right leg.

The volley of gunfire pierced the front of the building. Several shots pinged against the door and the wall of the conference room. But didn't penetrate the paneling. Another volley erupted along the side street. At least two cars. More shooters.

"Good idea. Just in case." Scott hit the floor. "I've never been in an armored car that was fired on."

"Now you tell us." Rafe grabbed Alison and shoved her down.

Doug scooted over to her. She was frozen in fright. Rigid paralysis. He cradled her body with his and felt her heart pounding.

Kara and Erik lay against the inner wall.

Doug kept a hold of Alison. She was stiff in his arms, and shaking.

The shots continued. Slamming into the building, breaking glass, splintering wood.

Then the lights and air conditioner went off. They'd hit the electricity. The room was plunged into darkness. Total darkness.

Alison whimpered. Doug rubbed his hand up and down her arm, trying to soothe her. Gradually the rigidity eased.

"Everything is being destroyed." Her words came out as a wail.

"Things, buildings, can be replaced. We're still alive."

A flashlight blazed. "I have more flashlights, and a lantern," Scott said. "I'll give us more light when the firing stops."

Alison stayed in Doug's arms, stayed in his embrace. But she was coming back from wherever her fear took her. His own fear lessened. "Scott, you're a genius. They hit all four sides of the building."

"You didn't like that car of yours, did you, Alison?" Erik asked.

She shuddered in his arms. "I have insurance." Her words sounded almost normal.

"No sirens yet. I'm calling this in." Rafe reached up and grabbed his phone. "I doubt our cop escorts are still alive out there." He called 911, reported the strafing.

The room was getting warm with the air conditioning off. It was going to be a sweltering July day. Beads of sweat formed on Doug's brow. From the heat or the tension?

The shooting went on and on for another minute, then stopped abruptly. "I'm thinking at least four shooters," Rafe said. "That's an awful lot of firepower."

"I was thinking the same thing." Doug's gut clenched. The noise was deafening.

Sirens sounded in the distance, coming their way. That's

why the shooting had stopped. The vehicles roared away. At least two of them. He couldn't tell.

The bullet proof paneling had held. A huge wave of relief sped through him.

"Remind me to give you a raise and a bonus, Scott." Doug sat up, keeping his hold on Alison. "On second thought, I won't need a reminder. We're all still alive."

"For now." Alison pulled out of his arms and scooted away.

He let her go. "They haven't beat us yet. And they're not going to."

"Cop killing is not going to help them." Scott's voice oozed venom.

Erik stood. "Judging from the number of shots, I'm not sure I want to see how many holes are in the building. I hope it can be patched."

"Anything can be fixed. Or rebuilt." Doug looked at all that had been saved. Along with their lives. "We'll be back in business here soon. For now, though, we're going to have to move to Jake's."

"When the police are finished with us," Alison said. "That may take a while." She rose from the floor and looked down at him, probably wondering if she could help him.

The sirens stopped outside and Doug swung his legs around, looking for a way to get up from the floor without embarrassing himself. Rafe and Scott saw his dilemma and grabbed his arms and pulled him to his feet.

"Thanks, guys. I didn't have the strength." Times like these his limitations really bothered him.

The back door splintered. Someone had kicked it in. Doug heard the wood coming apart.

"Doug? Anyone alive in here?" Panic in Nick's voice coming from the hallway.

"We all are," Doug called. "In the conference room."

Nick appeared in the doorway, a shocked look on his face. "I was sure it was going to be a blood bath in here. How?" He stood with his mouth open.

"Scott saved us."

Nick looked at Scott. "What magic wand did you wave?" He looked at the walls. "Bulletproofing?" His tone was incredulous.

Scott smiled. "Figured it might help us in a pinch. We got pinched."

Nick glanced at Doug. That shocked look still on his face.

"I've already told him he gets a raise and a bonus. His planning saved our lives."

"What about the guys outside?" Rafe asked. "Our escorts."

"They didn't have a chance. Mowed down in their cars." Nick walked into the center of the room and looked around. "No shots got through?"

"Not a one." Doug picked up his cane and limped toward the door.

Chet and two officers appeared at the door. They had expected a blood bath too. The looks on their faces were priceless. Doug smiled. They'd beat the odds.

"Bulletproofing on the walls," Nick said.

Chet shook his head. "For now, I want all of you to stay inside here. In case Moreno has someone watching to see how many of you were killed."

"Maybe his ego won't let him think we might have survived." Doug smiled. "We need to keep him in the dark as much as possible."

"Alison, you won't ever drive that car again," Chet said. "They made sure it was totaled."

Nick and Chet headed out of the room and Doug limped after them. They did a tour, assessing the damage.

"You won't be working here for a while," Nick said.

"We'll go to Jake's house."

"How long before he finds us there?" Alison said, coming up behind them.

Doug turned and pulled her into his arms, holding her close. "We're going to win. He's losing control. There's nothing methodical or rational about his moves today. Or yesterday."

He looked at Nick and saw the surprised look on his face. And let go of Alison. Though he didn't want to. She seemed to realize what had happened too, that they were drawn together instinctively, for comfort. She scooted back to the conference room.

He watched her go. They'd survived another attack. And a big step had been taken today. She let him hold and soothe her. Where it would lead, he had no way of knowing. Or if they would continue to survive Moreno's attacks.

ALISON PUSHED AWAY from the conference table and stared at the paneled walls that had saved their lives. Six survivors sitting around, numb, realizing how lucky they were.

Chet appeared at the doorway. "Okay, you're cleared to go. How many cars are drivable?"

Alison grimaced. "Not mine." Her stomach knotted, spreading tightness throughout her entire body. Was there a bullseye on her back? The attack at Dave's. The attack at the agency. Her car destroyed. Kenny coming.

Was it time for her to get out?

Leave the agency? Leave Doug? Leave the danger?

She glanced at Doug. He was watching her from the other side of the table.

If she were to run, she'd have to do it today. Before anything else happened. Before she found herself in Doug's arms again. Before she completely fell in love with him.

"Scott's car didn't make it." Nick joined Chet in the doorway. "It was on the street behind the unmarked car that probably took the first hit."

"I have a car up the street that may be okay." Doug stood and picked up his cane. "A tan Subaru."

Nick glared at him. "You aren't supposed to be driving."

"I haven't been. I had my mechanic park it there for emergency use. This is an emergency."

Alison caught the spark that flashed between the two men. She'd have to remember to ask Doug. She'd seen it before. Something unresolved from their past?

"So, four cars." Chet pulled out his phone. "I'll get four more regular patrol cars here for escort duty. Those goons won't be going near a patrol car. They should be miles away." He made the call and asked that the officers come in with sirens, that we'd be inside until they were here.

Chet pointed at Scott. "Go with Kara. You two are first. Wait for the siren, then go out."

"I'll escort Alison and Doug to Doug's car," Nick said. "They can go second. Then Erik, then Rafe."

Alison gathered her things, her laptop, briefcase, all her notes. Everything she'd brought into the conference room. No sense even checking her office. Nothing would have survived.

The first and second patrol cars arrived almost simultaneously. "Let's go." Nick picked up Doug's briefcase with his laptop and they headed to the destroyed back door.

Scott went through the door first, followed by Kara. "Do you want me to have this place boarded up later today?" He pulled open what was left of the door.

Doug limped outside. "Yes. To keep vandals out, when the police are finished. Do you have a firm in mind to do the job?"

"Always." Scott grinned. "I'll call them as soon as I get to Jake's. Chet, would you let me know when the crime scene is released so the crew can go to work?"

"Will do," Chet said. "Good thinking."

Alison followed Nick and Doug out the door. Doug pulled his car keys out of his pocket and was ready with the door opener when they approached the Subaru.

"Hand controls," Nick said. "An older car of yours?"

"I had it in storage, in case I needed it. My SUV is in storage now. It didn't burn in the fire."

"I was wondering why there was no mention of a vehicle in the arson report," Nick said. "You're a crafty one."

"Just being cautious."

Alison slid into the passenger seat and Doug got in and started the car.

"Be careful, both of you." Nick tapped the car in farewell and stepped back. Alison saw respect in his eyes this time.

Doug pulled away from the curb. A self-contented smile on his face.

"You're happy to be driving again."

"I don't like feeling helpless. Driving is something I can do. Running is not. I know my limitations."

She turned around in her seat and glimpsed the patrol car right behind them. No attempt to be coy. It was a distinct warning. Don't mess with the car in front of me. She felt more secure than she had in a long time.

Doug pulled into the driveway at Jake's and parked close to the back door, out of sight from the front. The patrol car saluted with a quick squeal of the siren as it pulled away.

They went inside through the back door and into the dining room. Alison put Doug's briefcase and her own on the table.

Scott came from the hallway. "Let's set up a safe room in this house. In the den. I'll have the guys panel all four walls and the door and cover the window with the bullet proofing material. We know it works. It could save us here too."

They followed him into the den.

Alison glanced around. "As long as we could get in here quickly. Ten people can't stay in here all the time."

"I hope the owner has good insurance. I'll ask Jake if the DEA arranged for renter's insurance. I'll also beef up the agency liability policy." Doug grimaced. "This lovely house could be destroyed."

"So much damage. So much destroyed already." Alison felt sorry for everyone having to fix the damage that had been done to so many places.

"The living room is not safe," Scott said. "And that's where, Dani, Sabrina, and Gracie are right now, watching a movie. Dave's upstairs on watch."

They went back out and into the living room. The trees and bushes outside the windows blocked anyone from seeing in, unless they came into the yard. Not likely. These guys wouldn't get that close. It was hit and run with them.

Erik and Rafe came in the back door. "Let's eat. It's past lunchtime," Erik said.

Sabrina bounced up from the couch and greeted Rafe with a quick kiss. Alison felt herself blushing. They were truly suited for each other.

"We've eaten," Sabrina said. "Sit down at the table and I'll bring in the food and you can help yourselves."

"I'll help you." Alison followed Sabrina into the kitchen.

"Thanks." Sabrina grasped her arm. "I'm so glad you all are

safe. Rafe called me right away, before we saw it on the news." She opened the refrigerator door and took out several bowls.

Alison grasped the bowl Sabrina handed to her. "How are you and Gracie and Dani doing?"

"The girls are scared. We watched the noon news, and saw the video about the attack on the agency. Even though we knew about the conference room walls, and knew from Rafe's call that you were okay, it was still tough to watch. I'd like to take the girls somewhere safer."

"I think that can be arranged. Betty needs to go too, whether she wants to or not. I'll talk to Doug about it after lunch."

"Talk to me about what?" Doug limped into the kitchen, grabbed a glass and filled it with water.

"Getting Sabrina and the girls and your mother out of town right away before anything else happens."

"I'll call my mother after lunch. Any ideas where you're like to go, Sabrina?"

"How about far away. On a plane." She removed the lids from bowls of various meats and salads.

Doug smiled. "You are desperate. I do know how much you don't like planes."

Sabrina met his smile with one of her own. "I am desperate. For the girls' safety. Anywhere far away."

"Oh, yes. That's a given," Doug said. "I'll figure something out. You'll be out of here early in the morning. That's a promise."

Alison found the stack of paper plates, the heavy duty ones, and counted out enough for the group. "And we can all hope nothing else happens tonight. This day has been too much."

"You were in two buildings that were strafed with gunfire." Doug's voice showed surprise, like he'd just realized it. "In the midst of everything happening, I'd forgotten that little fact. No wonder you were traumatized."

"I was paralyzed with fear. I've never felt such panic, ever."

"Do you want to go too? You can. Guilt free. You've been through enough already."

She thought about it. Thought about Doug's legs and how he needed someone by his side at all times. Thought about her own growing feelings for him. And in that instant, she'd made her decision. "No. I'm staying. Send Kara with them. She's still freaking out."

"Okay. That will work. Someone should be along who knows what to watch for. And I'll use the secret corporate identity to book flights and hotel rooms. And give Kara a corporate card for expenses."

Her gaze locked with his. "All we have to do is get through this night without another disaster."

CHAPTER 17

*A*s soon as lunch was over, Doug picked up his cell phone and called his mother. Sabrina started to leave the room, but he waved her into a seat. "This concerns you too."

His mother answered right away. "Doug, you're okay." Panic infused her words. "I saw the noon news. The building all full of bullet holes."

His heart clenched. Of course she'd be watching the news. "I'm sorry. I should have called sooner."

"Was anyone hurt? Did you all get out alive?"

"Everyone is fine. The building is a mess, as you saw. We were in a room behind bulletproof barriers."

"You were inside there all the time?" She was shouting. He instantly regretted telling her the truth.

Alison sat in the chair next to him, her closeness showing her concern. She obviously realized the reaction his mother would be having. She put her hand on his arm. The comfort was welcome.

"Yes, we were inside. But we were okay, just scared a little." He tried to downplay it for her benefit.

"I guess you're used to guns and bullets now." This time her voice relayed disgust.

He let that go. "The reason I called is to beg you to go on a trip. Far away. Before something else happens."

"What if I went to Hawaii? Would that be okay?"

"Perfect. Why Hawaii?" She must be scared too.

"Jeanette has a condo on Maui and we could go there."

"How big is the condo? How many people would it sleep?"

"Jeanette says ten. Does someone else need to get away? Dani, maybe?"

"Sabrina and Gracie too, and Kara for protection. Nick might want Tricia to go too."

"Oh, yes. That would be fine. We already talked about the possibility that more people might want to go." She hesitated. "Please come too." Her words and tone pleaded.

"I can't. This won't be over until Moreno is caught. He'll always be after me. And I can't stay away forever."

"But I'm so worried about you."

"And I'm worried about you and the young girls that are here. Can you be ready very early tomorrow morning?"

She asked Jeanette the question. "Yes, we can be ready."

"Someone will pick you up there at the house."

"Okay, what time?"

"I'll get back to you about a time, after I book the flights. I'll do that right now."

"I'll start packing and wait for your call. Thanks, Doug. We'll take good care of the girls. And I'll get to meet my grand-daughter and get to know her. This will be a fun trip."

"I'm glad it's going to work out for all of you. Take care and I love you." He ended the call and put down the phone.

"That was easy." Alison removed her hand from his arm. He'd been surprised she'd kept it there that long.

"She's finally realizing the danger." He turned to Sabrina. "How does Maui sound?"

"Really? We're going to Hawaii tomorrow?"

"Yes. Go tell the girls and have them start packing up what they have here. If any of you need more clothes when you get over there, you can go shopping. Kara will pay with the credit card I'm going to give her."

"Going home now to pack extra clothes wouldn't be wise, would it?" Sabrina perked up. "We'll be fine."

"Don't hesitate to get what you need over there."

"Okay." She got up from the table and headed to the living room.

"Where is Kara?" He turned to Alison.

"I saw her head upstairs after lunch. Do you want to talk to her now?"

"I guess I'd better make sure she'll go to Hawaii before I book her a flight."

Alison headed upstairs.

He opened his laptop and looked at flight schedules while waiting for Kara. Several possibilities for tomorrow. It would work.

"You wanted to talk to me?" Kara appeared at the doorway.

"Come sit down."

Kara sat at the table with him, her eyes wary.

"I need you do to a bodyguard job for a while."

Her eyes widened.

"I'm sending you to Hawaii with my mother, her friend, Sabrina, and the girls. And maybe Tricia. Is that okay with you?"

Her mouth hung open. "Uh, okay? Yes, I'll go to Hawaii as a

bodyguard for them. Gladly." She glanced around like she was afraid something awful was going to happen.

"Good. Be ready to leave very early tomorrow morning. I'm going to book the flights now."

Kara stood, looked back at him, "Thanks. I'd like to get away from here for a while."

"I figured you would. Go get packed. Do you have your gun case with you here? So you can check your gun through?"

"No. It's at my apartment."

Alison stood in the doorway. "Mine is upstairs. I'll loan it to you. Then you can check your gun through in your luggage." They headed for the stairs.

He picked up his phone and called Nick first, and got his okay to send Tricia along. Then called his travel agent, gave her detailed instructions and the list of names, and waited for a confirmation call.

It felt good being back in control. Making things happen instead of reacting. He wanted to keep that feeling.

His phone rang. Chet told him the crime scene was released. He limped into the den and found Erik and Rafe, sitting on the couch, watching Scott on a ladder with a measuring tape. "Rafe, use your van and the two of you go back to the agency and bring the computers and anything else you can salvage. Anything not destroyed."

"Sure." Rafe bounced up from the couch. "Beats sitting around here. Sabrina told me the women are heading for Hawaii tomorrow. Thanks."

They went out the back door.

Doug watched Scott for a few minutes. "Will your guys be able to do the job today?"

"They're on their way now." Scott came down from the ladder. "I was making some last minute calculations. Gus says he has enough material on hand. He was pleased that the paneling saved our lives."

"The agency building is ready for the security company to board it up, so give that crew the go-ahead too."

He returned to the dining room, which seemed to be his office temporarily, until the den was ready. He sat at his spot at the head of the table, by the window with a view of the backyard and the parking area. He took his gun out of the shoulder holster, set it on the table, covered it with a newspaper. Easy to grab. Then he downloaded email while he waited for Nick and Jake. Nick had told him they were on their way with pictures.

In ten minutes they joined him at the table.

Nick looked at him with an expression that surprised Doug. Sincere respect. "Thanks for including Tricia in the trip."

"She's family. So are you now."

Nick gazed at him a moment longer, then opened a folder and took out a large glossy photo and laid it on the table in front of Doug. "This is Kenny."

Alison was right. Kenny looked like any other Hispanic male.

"And here's Moreno and Armando." Jake set those two photos next to Kenny.

He studied Moreno first. "Not much change from the last time I saw him, about ten years ago. Some gray in his hair. He's about my age, maybe a couple years older. Which would make him about fifty."

"That's what the DEA files say is his age," Jake said. "They've kept track of him for many years, though they've only been building a case against him for three years."

"I don't understand why he isn't off the streets."

"He's an American citizen." Jake picked up the picture. "His mother gave birth in El Paso, then slipped back over the border into Mexico after his birth was registered."

"So quick deportation doesn't work with him," Nick said.

"Where was Armando born?" Doug picked up the next photo and saw the family resemblance. He was his father's son.

"In Los Angeles," Jake said. "Juanita Padilla, Moreno's former mistress, is his mother. When Moreno married, she took Armando and went home to Mexico, to her family."

"So Armando was several years older than Tomas and Miguel."

"Yes," Jake said. "Moreno married Carmen Herrera after Armando was born. She was American born and had money and connections."

"We're checking for any family here in Portland," Nick said. "So far we've come up with one distant cousin. We're watching his house."

"What about Enrique's family?" Doug asked. "He was picked up."

"He's being held on a warrant," Nick said. "But he was just one of the gang. Not living here anywhere. And he hasn't told us where he was staying."

"Getting to Moreno through the family may be what we have to do," Doug said. "But that's slow going. We don't have much time."

"Yeah," Nick said. "There's no let up on the pressure. Six days since this wave of violence started."

"Seems like longer." Doug shook his head.

"For you. You're the one living through this hell he created." Nick frowned and leaned back in his chair.

"And we have one other headache developing." Doug picked up the photo of Kenny Driscoll and studied it. "This loser wants revenge, for a shot in the shoulder and a stint in prison."

"Alison winged him?" Nick took the photo.

"He beat her up and broke her left arm, so she grabbed a gun she'd hidden and balanced it on the bed and fired one shot. It hit Kenny in the shoulder and stopped him. Then the police barged in. The neighbors had called 911."

"And Kenny went to prison, vowing revenge." Nick scowled and handed the photo back to Doug.

"Said he'd hunt her down and slice her to ribbons. He carries a switchblade." He studied the photo again. "Since he has the agency address, he could have followed any of us when we retreated here. He has no reason to be afraid of patrol cars yet."

"He wouldn't be relying on media information, like Moreno," Nick said. "He could have been watching the building, after the shooters left. Waiting to find out for himself if there were survivors."

Doug's gut clenched. "He could already know where she is."

CHAPTER 18

*A*lison found Doug alone in the dining room. "Was that Nick and Jake I heard?"

"They brought pictures."

"Pictures?" She slid into the chair next to him. He gazed at her, those dark brown eyes of his holding a promise.

"You and I have so much to talk about, that doesn't include these clowns. He pushed the pictures in front of her. "Kenny, Moreno, and Armando."

She held his gaze a moment longer, not wanting to think about Kenny. But she had to. A shudder ran the length of her body. She glanced at his picture, and her hands started to shake. "He looks mean. I don't know what I ever saw in him."

"You were a different woman. You've developed strength now that you didn't have. You don't have to settle for what's available. You have choices."

She looked at him again and wondered if there was a hidden meaning behind his words. Would she be settling, if she decided Doug was the man for her? No. He had strengths far superior to anything Kenny ever had. His crippled legs meant nothing. He was twice the man Kenny was.

The back door opened and Doug glanced out the window. "Kenny's here." He growled the words, then lifted the corner of the newspaper to show her his Beretta.

Nick and Jake appeared at the dining room doorway, followed by Kenny, with a gun trained on them.

Alison's heart squeezed, cutting off her oxygen. He'd found her. He was holding Nick's Glock and had another pistol tucked into his waistband. She took several ragged breaths, trying to clear her head. Was he going to kill them all?

"Over there, on that side of the table. Sit." Kenny motioned with the gun barrel.

Jake and Nick did as they were told. At least the gun was no longer at Nick's back.

"Hey you, cripple. Move around to that side of the table." He waved the gun barrel at Doug." I want the three of you lined up where I can mow you down if this bitch doesn't follow instructions."

Doug glanced at her, held her gaze for moment, then edged around to the chair next to Nick.

"Hands on the table. All of you. You too, bitch."

Alison put her hands on the table. They were shaking harder now.

"Okay, bitch. You and me are going for a ride."

She started to get up. Doug reached over and stopped her. "You're not going anywhere with that bastard."

"I'll take her where I want." Kenny's tone was taunting. "You're a cripple. You can't stop me. I seen you walk. You couldn't catch anyone."

Kenny glared at Alison. "Can't you do any better than a cripple? Are you that desperate for a man? Maybe I better keep you alive for a few days."

Cold chills climbed her spine. She glared right back at him. "This is Doug Landreth, my boss." She croaked out the words.

"It's his building got shot full of holes this morning? Someone besides me is after you." He laughed. A raw chuckle.

"Who else is here? This is a big house for two people."

"I don't live here," Alison said.

"Who does. Who lives here?" He bellowed the words.

"I live here. I'm renting the place." Jake words dripped with menace.

Kenny stared at him. "Who are you?"

"Jake Wilson. DEA. Federal law enforcement." He said it proudly.

"And you?" He looked at Nick.

"Detective Nick Castellani, Portland Police Bureau. And that's my service weapon in your hand. You're digging yourself a fast track back to San Quentin."

"Wow. I can bag me a cop, a fed, and a PI. Unless Alison leaves with me now."

Alison's heart squeezed tighter. She'd put them all in jeopardy by staying instead of running. She stared at Kenny and moved her right hand closer to the newspaper. Could she get a shot off before anyone got killed? That Beretta was so close. Also a huge risk.

A truck rumbled up the driveway and stopped behind the house.

"Who's coming?" Kenny demanded.

"Workmen. We have a renovation project going on," Jake said. "I need to get the door."

"No you don't." Kenny turned the gun toward him.

Someone pounded on the back door. "Scott, where are you?" a voice shouted.

"Who's Scott?" Kenny glanced around. "Where is he?"

"Right here." Scott yelled from the hallway. Then he threw something into the living room. It bounced against the coffee table.

Kenny's head turned.

Alison reached under the newspaper, gripped the Beretta, and fired two shots center mass. Aimed at his heart. Kenny crumpled to the floor and blood pooled beneath him. She lowered the weapon, though a strong compulsion to fire more shots into his body was almost overpowering.

Her hands were steady when she fired the weapon, but started shaking again as a heavy chill enveloped her. She stifled the urge to scream obscenities at him, the way he'd done after knocking her down.

Nick and Jake rushed to Kenny. Nick grabbed his Glock and Jake took the other weapon from his waistband. Nick checked Kenny's pulse. "He was dead before he hit the floor."

Doug scooted back to the chair next to Alison. He took the Beretta out of her hands and set it on the newspaper, then reached for her. She went willingly into his arms, burying her head against his chest. Shaking uncontrollably.

The pounding on the back door was louder. Scott opened the door and the two men who had installed the paneling at the agency came in. "What's going on?" one man asked. "Who got shot?"

"An attempted kidnapping," Scott said. "Thanks for being timely. You distracted him. Avert your eyes when you come through. Lots of blood."

"All in a day's work for you guys?" the other man said. "I saw the agency building after it was shot up. I'm glad the paneling saved your lives."

"So are we. Think of all this as movie material," Scott said. "We have two revenge plots playing out. One just finished." He gestured to the body on the floor. "We have to get ready for the other one that's still developing. Follow me." They went into the den.

Scott's attempt at humor helped Alison. She sat up straight and Doug relaxed his grip on her. She looked down at the newspaper, keeping her eyes diverted so she wouldn't look at Kenny. She didn't want to see what those two bullets did to him. The stuff of nightmares.

Dave came down the stairs, gun drawn. "I guess you didn't need my firepower. I would have taken him on."

"The jerk didn't know what he'd walked into." Doug stood and grabbed his cane. "Alison had the privilege of taking out her adversary. Neatly, quickly."

"Not neat, there's blood all over." Dave put his gun into his shoulder holster. "I'll go get something to cover him up." He ran up the stairs and returned with a blanket. He threw it over Kenny.

Alison glanced that way. He'd also stretched it out to cover most of the blood. She took a big breath to bring down her heart rate. She could handle this. Kenny was gone. He'd never bother her again.

Nick called 911 and reported the shooting and asked for a quick resolution of the crime scene, since he saw it all. And the suspect was dead.

"The crime scene people will want everyone out of this area of the house while they process the scene," Nick said.

"Everyone who isn't needed by the police can go to a hotel

suite for a while," Doug said. "I have three reserved, in case of emergency. I'd say this warrants using at least one of them."

Alison stood. "Could Kara and Sabrina and the girls stay in one tonight?"

"Good idea. One is out by the airport. Go upstairs and tell them to get their stuff together and bring it down. They can go immediately, if they're ready."

Alison went up the stairs and found all four of them huddled together in Kara's small room.

"All under control," she said. "That was Kenny, my ex, who wanted me dead. He's the one dead now."

"Who shot him?" Kara asked.

"I did. Doug had a gun concealed under a newspaper." And she realized she'd really done it. Stood up for herself.

"What happens now," Sabrina asked.

"The four of you are going to spend the night in a hotel suite near the airport and go to the airport from there in the morning," Alison said. "Are you packed? How soon can you be ready to go to the hotel?"

"I'm ready now," Dani said. "I don't like all this shooting."

"I'm ready," Gracie said. "Ready to get out of here."

Alison felt sorry for the girls, for the wide-eyed terror on their faces. They would never forget these days.

"Five minutes," Sabrina said. She went back to her own room.

"When we go downstairs, walk through the hall and dining room without looking at the body on the floor. He's covered with a blanket, but there's a lot of blood." She watched the girls for a reaction. They nodded their heads. They understood.

Alison helped them take their bags downstairs and out to Sabrina's van. It took all her willpower to keep from glancing down at Kenny. At what remained of the threat that had been held over her head for such a long time. Some of that great weight began to lift. Now all they had to do was take care of Moreno. A tougher job. Kenny was a two-bit criminal. Moreno was a pro.

ALISON SAT at the head of her bed, propped up by pillows, and stared out the window at the trees behind the house. Looking at everything. Looking at nothing.

Kenny's body was gone. The crime scene people had left. The worst of the blood had been removed. A cleanup crew was downstairs tackling the stains left behind.

The tap of Doug's cane sounded on the hardwood floor in the hallway. Then a soft knock on the door. Did she want to talk to him? Or did she want to be alone?

She hesitated a moment. "Come in. It's not locked."

He pushed open the door and stopped in the middle of the room. "Are you okay?"

"I'm alive. Kenny's dead. I guess that means I'm okay."

"No, I'm asking about your emotional state. Are you going to be able to put this behind you? Or do you need to go away to grieve?"

"Grieve for Kenny?" She thought about it. "Yes, I guess I am grieving right now. I'm questioning the meaning of life. How things can go so wrong for some people."

Doug limped over to her and sat on the edge of the bed, laying his cane across the end. He turned his body so he was looking at her. He was close enough that he could have touched her, but he didn't.

Doug on the same bed with her. She felt that little dance of nerves. Would she ever experience making love with this man? Did she want to?

Hell, yes. If the right opportunity arose.

He reached out his hand. She joined her hand with his. Felt the rough surface. A man's hand was never smooth.

"Do you want to go to Hawaii tomorrow too? I can arrange it."

"No. I can't leave you. I want to be here for the showdown with Moreno."

"That's taking a risk." The look in his eyes was mesmerizing. Was he getting turned on sitting close to her? On the bed?

"Life's a risk. What we do for a living is a risk. Our traumatic pasts put us at risk." Caring for you is a risk.

He gripped her hand tighter. "Are you willing to take another risk? With your heart? Are you willing to get to know me as a man instead of a boss?" The look in his eyes told her this was very important to him. He was having the same thoughts she was.

Did she dare risk problems later? Or throw caution to the wind and grab what happiness she could right now? "I don't know what I want. I was so focused for years on avoiding Kenny, hiding from him, that I didn't dare think about another relationship."

"I know what you mean. After Patti was killed and I was injured, I pretty much thought my life was over. A desk job somewhere, but no involvement with another woman. I was too risky for her."

She laughed. "Here I am risking my life alongside you, and it's both of us protecting the other. The gun under the newspaper."

"That's what partnerships are all about. That's what relationships are all about too. Mutual care and caring for the other."

She pulled her hand out of his grip. "You've been thinking about this lately."

He kept his eyes focused on hers. "I've had a lot of time to think about it. These are strange times."

"Blip on the radar. The building will be restored, your house will be rebuilt, your mother's house will be renovated. And the agency business will go on as before."

"You're forgetting one thing. Moreno isn't finished with us. With me."

"What are you asking? That we take another risk, that we grab what we can now?"

He shifted on the bed, bringing his legs up onto the comforter. Moving closer to her. "I'm not trying to rush you into anything. I'm just saying I'm interested, if you are. We can leave it at that for now."

"I'm confused."

"As anyone would be who'd been through two attacks with assault rifles and was almost kidnapped and killed."

"It has been an eventful few days." She gazed into his dark eyes, at the passion in them.

"And I shouldn't have brought up the subject yet. I should have waited."

"No. You've given me a glimpse of hope. That life can normalize. That my future isn't necessarily bleak. That I can be with a man again without fear."

"Then we'll leave it at that. As a possibility for the future. After Moreno is no longer a threat."

She felt a sudden loss. Maybe she didn't want to wait. She leaned forward. Doug must have seen something in her eyes. He reached out and pulled her closer and their lips met. She grasped his shoulders and let herself feel his kiss.

Tingling sensations suffused her entire body. Her taut

nerves came alive and her senses soared. She was flying. His lips moved on hers and she opened up. He deepened the kiss. She wanted closer, wanted more. Her heart rate accelerated.

He pulled back. Breathing hard. "I guess that wasn't a good idea. Too many people in this house for us to see where this leads."

She took a deep breath, to calm her own breathing. And took another risk. "It will happen when the time is right."

He stared at her and smiled. "When the time is right."

His smile held such promise.

He scooted to the edge of the bed and stood. Then grabbed his cane. "I'd better summon the troops and see where we stand. Get back to the business of trying to stay alive." He smiled again, that captivating smile she was seeing more often. "So we can enjoy the future."

"Thanks for coming upstairs. I do feel better now." She felt herself blushing.

"Come on down when you're ready. You don't have to rush." He left the room.

She sat on the edge of the bed. What had she done? Risked her future job security for a fling with the boss? Or risked her heart for a chance at a secure relationship?

CHAPTER 19

*W*hat if they ran out of luck? Doug limped out of the den, to the kitchen, where he put his paper plate in the trash and his fork in the sink. Four of them in the den, hiding while eating their dinner. Dave ate upstairs at the front window. Rafe ate at the window that looks out on the backyard and the back gate. Jake was still with Nick.

Doug glanced into the living room, then advanced into the room. A nice, comfortable place. Off limits. The dining room behind him. Off limits. Shots fired at the front of the house would go all the way through to the dining room. The bushes that shielded the front windows would be ripped apart by the bullets.

He pulled out his cell phone and called Chet.

"Any chance we could get SERT coverage 24/7, since Moreno's hoods took out those cops? We need the extra protection, before it's too late."

"I'm fighting the powers that be," Chet said. "And another car drove past the agency ten minutes ago and put holes in the plywood on the front and side."

"Strike me down, then hit me again. That seems to be their mode." He settled onto the couch, to rest his leg.

"Since no casualty numbers have been released, they've figured out they didn't get anybody yet."

"And now they're frustrated even more. Anything could happen." Doug let his own frustration show in his words.

"How many of you are at the house now?"

"Seven, counting Jake when he gets back. The women and girls fly out to Hawaii in the morning. They're at a hotel at the airport."

"Good. I'm going to keep hassling the lieutenant until I get you SERT coverage. Might not be tonight. I'll let you know when I have confirmation."

"Thanks." He ended the call.

"What are you doing out here?" Alison appeared at the edge of the living room. "You're taking a chance."

"I called Chet. Asked for SERT coverage." He stood and held out his hand.

"Will we get it?" She moved toward him, hesitated, then took his hand.

"He's working on it. It won't happen immediately. We'll have to get through the night and get the women and girls off to Hawaii in the morning."

He pulled her into his arms and settled her against his chest. She started to resist, then relaxed and let him hold her. "Damn. I want Moreno captured. I want a chance to see where this leads. I want to be with you."

She stiffened. He ran his hand down her back, caressing her until she relaxed again.

"I won't rush you." His whole body screamed for more, for

another kiss. To make love to her. To hold and cherish her. To make her his. He was sure that hiding inside her cool exterior was a passionate woman. He wanted to explore that passionate connection between them.

He didn't want to wait until some mythical time in the future when everything was peaceful. He needed her now, needed her beside him, needed the connection. She completed him and made him feel like a whole man. When he was with her, his wanting turned into a fierce desire.

He heard her soft sigh. For now he'd have to be satisfied.

"We could have a future together." He whispered the words.

She pulled away. "I'm not sure I'm ready." She glanced at the spot on the floor where Kenny had fallen and died. Her face lost its glow.

Too soon. He should have waited. "I meant it when I said I won't rush you. All I'm asking is that you give us a chance."

"I'll think about it."

He followed her to the door of the den, then opened the door. Her expression was guarded.

She sat on the couch.

Doug set down his cane, then joined her on the couch. Keeping a discreet distance between them. Wanting so much more than she was ready to give.

He ignored Scott's inquiring gaze and opened his laptop to download his email.

The back door opened. Doug's hand automatically went to his gun in his shoulder holster.

"It's me. Jake." He opened the den door and poked his head in.

Doug frowned and let his hand drop back to his lap. He was definitely edgy.

Jake walked in and closed the door. "Cozy in here." The words didn't sound like a compliment.

"Can't be helped," Scott said.

Erik paused with his hands on his keyboard. "I wish I could find a clue, something that would lead us to Moreno's country hideout."

Jake set his laptop on the coffee table and sat next to Doug. "Good news for a change. I had a talk with Hensley." He booted his laptop. "Hensley would like to keep a lid on things for a while longer. He's not willing to go for the capture yet. But he's willing to share information. After those two cops were killed."

"He has information that could help us find Moreno's hideout? And he's keeping it to himself?" Doug raised his voice.

"Not only him but the task force and his superiors. The attack on the agency woke everybody up. The finger pointing has started."

"It's about time," Alison said.

Jake pulled the table closer to the couch. "Everyone is ready to help you and the agency. Hensley realizes time is short. He's seen how much damage the gang has done in a few days."

"Nice of him to acknowledge that."

"Yeah, and I'm sorry I was a party to it. I've been authorized to give you everything I have and help you with searches that may locate Moreno's gang." He heaved a big sigh. "I'll make it up to you with hard work. I do want this agency to survive. You are a great bunch of people."

Doug studied him a moment. He seemed sincere. Two cops gunned down by gang violence at once. That was major for Portland. Undoubtedly the DEA was getting heat from the Police Bureau.

"Thanks, Jake. We do need the help. We have some gang members to catch and a massacre to avoid." And he'd be watching to see if Jake delivered.

"You could have all been killed this morning. Nick told me why you weren't. You're all professionals and Scott is the hero of the day."

"And now this room is paneled in bulletproof material," Doug said. "Scott engineered that job too."

"You haven't seen the best part." Scott got up and went to the window. It was covered so you couldn't see out. "Watch." He pulled a latch and slid the paneling and the window to the side, leaving a wide open space. "This is the escape hatch if the place is firebombed. And it's the most secure window in the entire house."

"What if we're upstairs?" Jake asked.

Scott slid the paneling back in front of the window. "The person on watch at the front bedroom window is behind bulletproofing, at the sides and bottom of the window, stretching five feet each side. So the only exposure is looking out the window."

"Which is the reason for being there," Doug said. "There is some risk. Dave's up there now."

"Also," Scott said, "there's a rope ladder in each room upstairs, secured to the floor, for a quick exit to the ground." He grinned. "That's what saved Doug's mother." Then he sobered. "But we need better latches on all the downstairs windows, just in case. I'll work on that problem tomorrow."

If we get through this night. Doug couldn't keep away that thought. "Okay, Jake. What can you tell us?" Doug gestured at Jake's open laptop. "What does the task force know that we don't?"

"For starters, the location of two houses in Portland where Moreno relatives live."

Erik scooted back to his computer. "Give me addresses."

"Better yet, I'm going to give you access to a database set up by the DEA for Moreno and his gang." Jake got up and went to the computer. Erik stood and let Jake have the chair and access to the keyboard.

Jake typed in an address and a password and opened a database.

Erik's eyes lit up. "Ramon Moreno—Family and Friends. Cool. Do we get the password?"

"I've been authorized to give it to you. But I was going to do it anyway tonight. I'm tired of hiding information you guys need." He wrote on a pad of paper Erik had left by the computer. "Here's the password and the URL of the database."

Doug was sure he saw guilt on Jake's face. That could mean Jake's full cooperation. Something they desperately needed.

Jake tapped a few keys and turned back to the room. "Here's Moreno's family tree, as accurate as DEA records and Mexican records could make it. Drug traffickers tend to use family as much as they can. The loyalty factor."

"Now we can go on the offensive," Doug said. "We not just targets."

"What do you mean, go on the offensive?" Jake stood and faced Doug.

"When we, or the officers hunting the killers of the two cops, locate the hideout, Moreno can be taken alive." Doug stood and leaned on his cane. "I'm no longer bait."

"You haven't been considered bait."

"I guess not. If Moreno or his goons were to come here to this house to kill me, the DEA wouldn't have any shooters out front, defending me."

"That's not the DEA role. We don't have SWAT type units. We rely on locals when extra firepower is needed."

"So we still have to depend on Portland's SERT to defend us. If they get here in time." He emphasized the last sentence. "Remember, those two cops are very dead."

"The DEA couldn't do anything about that."

"Yes they could have. They could have found Moreno and arrested him and stopped the violence. Long before he became so powerful. Long before he had my daughter killed. Long before he came to Portland to kill me."

"Like I've been telling you, they are gathering evidence that will stand up in court." Jake sat in the chair vacated by Scott, who was leaning against the outer wall, next to the covered window.

Erik's hands were still on the keyboard, but he'd stopped searching to watch Jake.

Doug glanced at Alison. Her head was down. She was staring at the floor.

Everyone wanted to know where Jake stood. Where his loyalties lay. Where his conscience would lead him.

Doug dropped back to the couch and laid down his cane. Jake's conscience was the key. When the shooting started.

CHAPTER 20

*A*lison warmed her hands around the steaming cup of coffee as the early morning sun bathed the backyard area in muted light. Three hummingbirds were feeding at a blue hydrangea bush outside the kitchen window. Another sunny warm day ahead after the chill of the morning wore off. And she should be in the den.

Her cell phone rang. The one in her left pocket. The one that hardly ever received a call. Except from her lawyer. She took it out of her pocket and looked at the number. Not her lawyer. Not a number she recognized.

She answered. "Alison Steele. Do I know you?"

"No. Eddie Velasquez told me to call you if I needed help."

Alison's gut twisted. The accent of a Hispanic woman. Could it be a trap?

"What kind of help?" She sat at the small table next to the window.

"I want to get away from Armando Moreno. But I'm afraid to leave the house. I have nowhere to go."

"What is your name and where are you?"

"I'm Mariana Perez. And I'm in Portland. Armando made me come. I don't want to be here." Her voice was shaky. Like she was scared. Or being told to call.

Alison grabbed a pad and pen from the counter and wrote down the name. "When did Velasquez give you my name and number?"

"After you left Los Angeles. In October. He said you were a good lady. A detective."

"Did you know Eddie was killed?"

"Yes. Moreno had him killed. Even bragged about it. That's why I'm scared."

"Are you being mistreated?"

Doug limped into the room. He raised a brow.

She added "woman from Armando's group" to the pad and showed it to him.

"I have to work hard. I don't want to be here, but I don't know how to get away from them." The voice did sound scared.

Alison weighed her options. It could be a legitimate call, or it could be a setup, to lure them out of hiding. "Can you get away during the day to meet with me?"

Doug moved closer, to try to hear the other side of the conversation. Alison held the phone out, so the sound would carry.

"I don't know. I can try."

"Are you a prisoner?"

"Armando makes us work all day. I cook and do laundry. And clean house."

"Does Armando sleep at that house?"

"No. But he comes every day to check on us. Ten people live here."

"Are you being watched?"

"I don't know. There's always people around, wanting food or something."

"Where are you? What part of Portland?"

"I'm in a house near Johnson Creek. They talked about the creek and how it floods sometimes."

"Have you been to that big mall on 82nd? Are you anywhere near 82nd Avenue?"

"I can't go anywhere. And I don't have any money."

"Can you walk outside the house?"

"I'm outside now, behind a big shed."

"I need the address of the house where you are. And the name of the street. Can you get that for me?"

"I can go out to the front yard when no one is looking. The house is on a corner and there are street signs."

"How are you calling me without anyone knowing?"

"I have a phone I bought in L.A. No one knows I have it."

"Don't let anyone see what you're doing. Call me back when you have the names of the streets. And the address. Okay?"

"Yes, I'll find out. As soon as I can."

"Be careful."

"I will. Goodbye."

Alison stared at the phone, frowning. Wondering about Mariana Perez.

Doug handed her the pad. "Your feelings. Is it a trap?"

"I don't think so. She did sound scared. And kind of hopeless. Like she feels she has to do something."

"Could be that Armando is maintaining that house in the Johnson Creek area for his own people but spending time with his father at the hideout in the country."

Rafe came through the back door, followed closely by Scott. "Packages delivered," Rafe said. "They looked very relieved to be leaving town. We stayed with them up to the checkpoint."

157

Scott looked around the kitchen. "What? No one has started breakfast?"

"Alison had an interesting phone call that may turn out to be helpful," Doug said. "A woman claiming Armando brought her to Portland and she doesn't want to be here."

"And how did she get Alison's phone number?" Rafe asked.

"From Eddie Velasquez," Alison said. "Back in October. Supposedly he told her that I could help her if she needed help."

"Sounds like a fishing expedition," Scott said. "She's trying to find out our location for Armando."

"Could be," Doug said. "Or this could be our lucky break."

Rafe opened the refrigerator and took out bacon and eggs. "Well, I'm hungry. I guess I have to feed the troops."

"I'm glad someone can cook around here," Scott said. "I certainly can't. But I can help."

"Are Jake and Erik here too?" Rafe asked. "And I assume Dave is still upstairs on watch."

"Yes," Alison said. "And Jake's at the back window. Erik is on the computer. Breakfast for seven. We'll get out of your way and let you two go to work." She refilled her coffee cup and filled one for Doug. They retreated to the den.

Alison sat on the couch. "What do we do if she calls back?"

Doug sat near a small table that held his laptop. "We need to find out where the house is located. Then we can do surveillance and see if Armando will lead us to the hideout."

"That could prove difficult. They know who we are."

"They don't know Erik yet."

"You're talking about me?" Erik swiveled in his chair.

"Just mulling ideas. How to follow Armando to the hideout." He told Erik about the call Alison received.

"We need that address," Erik said.

"If Mariana Perez can be trusted."

"I don't trust anyone right now, except agency people and the police. But we'll use her information if we can. And I'm not sure about the DEA."

"Jake's boss could be playing us along too?" Alison set her empty cup on the coffee table.

"He wants information about Moreno and his gang," Doug said. "Not to put him out of business. He wants to build that airtight case that he can use in court."

"After we're all dead." She had to add that. It had been on her mind. Constantly.

"I'll go check on breakfast and bring back the coffee pot." Erik left the room.

"The longer he's on the loose, the more damage he can do." Doug's eyes met hers and she felt the heat of his gaze. He was no longer thinking about Moreno or the young Hispanic woman.

"We have to do something to locate Moreno." She tried to distract him.

"I think we need to get away from this house for a while today. Find someplace private."

"And?" Her heart beat accelerated.

"See where it leads." He was searing her with that gaze.

"Is that safe?"

"Nothing is safe. Anything could happen. But they don't know where we are now." His words said one thing, his tone another.

"Do you think Moreno will be unhappy that they've lost track of us?"

"Definitely." Doug shook his head. "Moreno doesn't like loose ends. There will be problems. And I don't think all seven of us should stay here without going anywhere."

"Spread out the targets."

"Right. Chet called earlier. Wants me to meet with him and Nick. A lunch meeting at the airport hotel." He hesitated, like he wasn't sure of himself. "Then we could stay a little longer."

She gazed at him, at his masculine face and upper body. He was a prime specimen of a man, if you didn't look at his legs. She'd stopped doing that. She knew him for the man he was. He was offering respite from worry, and a chance to grab pleasure where they could. Maybe hope for a future together.

Rafe opened the door. "Breakfast. Come fill your plates. I'll take plates upstairs to Jake and Dave. Then Scott and I can relieve them on the windows after breakfast."

Alison ignored all the reasons why making love with Doug could go wrong. "Okay." Her gaze locked with his.

DOUG JOTTED some notes on a pad, his favorite way of thinking and planning. Alison refilled coffee cups, then sat in the chair next to the covered window. Her private phone sat on the small table near her.

Moments later the phone rang. She picked it up. "It's her." She waited until the room was quiet, then answered. She wrote something on the pad in front of her, then ended the call. "The house is on the corner of 77th Avenue and Harney Street. A white house with various garages and sheds on the property. And a lot of vehicles. A chain link fence around the whole property."

"I know that area," Doug said. "I was a cop in this town years ago. Before L.A."

"What's the set up for surveillance?" Jake set down his coffee cup

"Houses lining the streets. No open areas," Doug said. "A

car parked down the street is about the best we can do." He opened his laptop and booted it. Then clicked on Google Earth and located the house using the street names. "Here's the house." They each took a turn looking at the image on the screen.

Erik went back to his computer. "Not an area where people are walking around. No sidewalks."

"I have an idea," Jake said. "Will Siegel wants to help us. Going behind Hensley's back, essentially. He asked if there was anything he could do."

"And no one in the gang would recognize him?" Alison asked.

"He's new to the team. Hasn't worked down in Los Angeles."

Doug glanced again at the image on the screen. "He's willing to help us? Get this thing ended and Moreno out of business?"

"Like I said, he's seeing your side of it, rather than the strict DEA line. Since he's only been DEA for a short time, he chafes at the rigidity of the organization."

"Dave, why don't you go with Will to look over the situation. Find the house and see what's there now. See if it's any different. If it's okay with Will, I'd like him to do the daytime surveillance. Not one of us."

"I'll call Will and have him come here," Jake said. "Everyone needs to meet him."

"Good idea." Alison frowned. "I'm not sure I remember which one he was. That was a strange task force meeting."

Jake chuckled. "It was Hensley's way of trying to intimidate Doug. Obviously it didn't work." He went out of the den to make his call.

"Moreno is coming after me, not Hensley." Doug let the anger show in his tone. "I have a vested interest in how this whole thing unfolds. I intend to come out alive."

"I'd love to get one of those bastards in my sights." Dave simulated a gun in his hand, firing.

"Aren't you getting thoroughly bored sitting up there at that window?" Doug asked.

"Not at all. I like watch detail. It's quiet. I stare out the window."

"You don't have to do it all the time."

"I want to. I'm comfortable being by myself."

"But I think you enjoyed Dani's company."

"Ah, Dad is wondering what happened in my house."

Doug chuckled. "I trust you, Dave. But I don't know my daughter. And that's a fact."

"You need to get to know her. She's a neat person. I wouldn't mind getting to know her better. But I don't think she likes my biker dude persona."

"Oh?" He was surprised at the relief he felt. "Maybe she'll stick around after this messiness is over."

"And we're all still alive."

"I'm counting on staying alive. I have several very good reasons to survive."

Dave glanced at Alison. So did Erik. Alison blushed.

And Doug knew that what he planned was right, even if the timing was off.

Someone knocked at the back door. A couple of minutes later Jake opened the den door and Will Siegel followed him into the room.

"That was fast." Doug's hackles rose. Was Hensley having this house watched?

"I was already in the neighborhood. Hensley's idea," Will said. "I was willing, since I figured I could help you out too."

Will Siegel was tall, sturdily built. The kind of guy you wanted on your side in a fight. If it came to that. Doug hoped it wouldn't. They'd have to watch him, though. Watch for any surprises.

Jake handled the introductions.

Doug studied the newcomer. "We have a job for you, if you're willing. If you can leave here."

"I can," Will said. "Hensley just said to check out this place occasionally to see what was happening."

"Do you have any other assignment?"

"Database stuff. Find the rest of the group."

"We located one of their gang houses," Doug said. He watched Will's face for a reaction. Saw his raised eyebrow. He wasn't expecting them to score.

"Where?"

"Doug turned the laptop around so Will could see the image on the screen. "This is what it looks like on Google Earth."

"Not a secluded area. Not where Moreno is."

"No, but ten people live there now," Doug said. "Armando comes and goes but doesn't stay there."

"You do have information," Will said. "Someone on the inside?"

"A woman who doesn't want to be there. Sounds like domestic slavery to me."

"Will they catch her talking to you?"

"I hope not," Doug said. "I want Dave to go with you to take a look at the house, then bring him back and you get the job of surveillance during the day."

"I'll take the night shift if someone will loan me a car," Dave said. "They didn't see me, just my house when they shot it up."

"Are you sure," Doug asked. "You've been spending the days upstairs."

"Hey, this isn't going to last long. I can do anything for a short while."

"We all can. I'll take some watch time upstairs too, like this morning. I have a lunch meeting with Nick and Chet. Alison will go with me."

"I can take some shifts too," Jake said.

"I guess I'm the only one who doesn't shoot." Erik gestured toward his computer. "I'll stick with what I know."

"Alison sticks with me." Doug's words were emphatic. "She's my fire power to help even the odds."

"Is she good?" Jake's voice held a hint of doubt. "When the shot isn't point blank range?"

"She can out shoot all of us. I found her at the indoor range in Portland and recruited her for the agency. Yes, she's that good."

Alison blushed under his praise, but he meant every word. No one, not even him, could out shoot her.

Dave and Will left.

"Are you vouching for him, Jake?" Doug asked.

"He sounds sincere. He liked what you said at the task force meeting. He understands your position."

"So he'd stand with us against Hensley, if it comes to that?"

"If it comes to that," Jake said.

Trust two DEA agents? Right now he had no choice. Moreno was the biggest and most unpredictable problem. But the DEA had shown they were part of the problem.

CHAPTER 21

*B*y the time Doug arrived at the hotel coffee shop with Alison, he'd decided that the Police Bureau could also be part of the problem. Chet and Nick had become his watchdogs. They waited in a secluded booth in the darkest part of the coffee shop.

He had a funny feeling in the pit of his stomach as they followed the hostess to the dark corner. Chet and Nick sat on one side of the booth.

Alison slid in the other side and Doug sat next to her. Close, but not close enough. Whatever happened in this meeting, he had something to look forward to later. He greeted the men.

A hovering waitress quickly filled their coffee cups. Then took their orders for sandwiches. Doug certainly didn't care what he was eating. The others didn't seem to care either.

"Thanks for coming," Chet said. "This will be the last time you leave the house until this is over, and we won't be meeting with you there, unless the house becomes another crime scene."

Doug's gut tightened. "Who made that decision?" He didn't like being right.

The chief. He's pulling the escort cars and putting SERT on alert. He doesn't want any more dead cops."

"What about dead agency members?" Doug kept his tone neutral.

Alison set down her coffee cup. "If we have credible knowledge of an upcoming attack, will SERT protect us?"

"How would you find out about an attack?" Chet used a tone Doug had never heard from him before. He was being pressured and the agency would be the losers.

"We've located a gang house in southeast Portland." Doug studied Chet's face for a reaction. Just a quick frown.

"But no Moreno," Nick said. "Otherwise you'd be doing cartwheels."

"But maybe a way to find him," Alison said. "I got a call from a young woman in the house. She told me Armando is in and out but doesn't sleep there. Ten people live in the house."

"And you trust her?" Nick's tone was skeptical.

"Velasquez gave her my cell phone number before he died. She's scared and wants help getting away from Armando."

"Who's watching the house now?" Chet's tone carried censure.

Doug glared at him. "Will Siegel from DEA. Jake introduced us today. He's going to do the daylight surveillance. Dave volunteered for nighttime duty."

"Where is this house?" Again, demanding words.

"On the corner of 77th and Harney. Small house. Several outbuildings. Ten people would make it crowded." He kept his gaze on Chet.

"Typical of a gang house around here. Pull your guys and let the police and DEA do the surveillance."

"Will is DEA." Doug drained his coffee cup and signaled to that hovering waitress with the coffee pot.

"Sounds like he's freelancing," Nick said. "Hensley would not have allowed it."

"We need to locate where Moreno is hiding," Alison said. "Someone has to follow Armando. He's the key."

Doug reached for her hand and squeezed it. This meeting was what he expected, but they'd get through it and go upstairs.

Their sandwiches arrived. Doug picked up his ham and cheese and took a bite. Time to calm down.

Chet set down his sandwich. "Your people shouldn't be doing the surveillance. You're the targets."

"Are you being pressured by Hensley too?" Doug saw the flinch in Nick's jaw.

"Not pressured. But told to keep the lid on things," Chet said. "The task force is still trying to do the job they were formed to do."

"While they build that airtight case, Moreno will keep killing."

"So far just cops have died," Nick said. "That's what the chief is upset about."

Doug scowled at him. "So it would be okay if my people had died?"

"Maybe our luck won't hold," Alison said. "We've been a step ahead of him most of the time so far."

Doug reached for her hand again. "Think positive. We're going to survive and get rid of Moreno." He used his commander voice, rallying the troops voice. Alison was getting spooked. And she had reason to be.

Chet and Nick didn't respond. They didn't believe it either. They knew anything could happen.

"In other words, we are prisoners in the house." Doug

scowled. "We're not supposed to be proactive and go after Moreno. But if he comes after us, we can fight back. Is that how it is?"

"Yes," Chet said. "You have no authorization for a takedown unless it's self-defense."

"That ties our hands," Alison said. "Makes us sitting ducks."

"Keeps you inside the law," Chet said. "Keeps everything legal."

"Keeps us from adequately protecting ourselves." Doug let his exasperation show in his voice.

They finished their sandwiches and Chet stood. "Go back to the house. You'll have your escort that far, then he's leaving." They left, paying the bill on their way out.

Doug smiled at Alison. "Reminds me of the task force meeting. This time the message came from the Police Bureau. I'm the problem."

"So, what do we do?"

He gazed at her, at the soft blue of her eyes. "Our escort will have to wait a while."

She smiled back and he took that as a yes.

"I'll be right back." He went to the registration desk in the lobby and got a key for the room he'd reserved days earlier. He was in the mood to grab any vestige of happiness he could find. And Alison was that ray of hope.

ALISON WAITED for Doug at the entrance to the coffee shop. She couldn't miss his limp, as he came toward her, using his cane. He'd been walking too much again. But he wouldn't let up until Moreno was taken care of. At least he wasn't self-conscious about his limp. When he'd considered the alternative, him dead at the scene like his wife, he fully accepted his disability. It allowed him to continue living. And didn't diminish him as a desirable man.

He smiled at her, then held out his left hand. "Let's go make some memories."

She took his hand, his words vibrating through her body and settling into her feminine parts. That tingling sensation that developed when she was close to him.

He led her to the elevator. Another couple rode up with them, so he let go of her hand and kept his distance. But the vibes coming off his body left her with no doubt of his own arousal. Was she making a mistake going with him? Would making love with him change their working relationship?

She decided the risk was worth it. Her body had its own demands. And needs. She grasped his left arm for the walk down the hallway to the room. Heat pulsed through her hand and up her arm. Neither of them spoke. They both knew what they wanted.

Her breathing escalated and her heart pounded. Almost to the door.

He stopped in front of the door and smiled down at her. Then dipped his head for a quick kiss. Enough to take her breath away.

He opened the door and put his hand at the small of her back to usher her into the room. That tingling in her nerves escalated until she was sure her pounding heart could be heard by anyone nearby. Especially him.

"I'm forgetting something." Doug turned back to the door and put the "Do not disturb" sign on the outer door knob. Then double locked the door.

That tingling sensation revved up as his eyes devoured her.

The room had two queen sized beds. He tossed his cane

onto the far bed. It bounced off the other side, onto the rug. He kept his eyes locked with hers, not flinching or looking for the errant cane.

They stood two feet apart. "I've dreamed of this day ever since I first saw you at the range."

"And that's why you hired me?" She had to know the truth.

"No. I hired you for your shooting ability and your professionalism."

She didn't say anything.

"I've tried to fight my attraction to you. I can't fight it anymore. I need you."

"I never expected to want another man, after the last two jerks I ended up with. I thought they'd destroyed my trust in men completely."

"Are you ready for this?" Doug asked, a vulnerable look in his eyes. "Am I coming on too strong?" He shuffled forward and gripped her upper arms. But kept his body rigidly away from hers.

"I'm ready." She stared into his dark eyes and saw the melting of fear in them. He thought she might turn him down. Even after coming upstairs with him. Did she really have that kind of power over him?

"I'm really nervous. There's been no one since Patti."

"That makes two of us who are nervous. I don't want to fail to please you."

"You please me by being here with me. We can take it slow and see what develops."

She smiled.

"I'll show you my scars, if you show me yours." He had that silly grin on his face that showed his embarrassment. Or was he feeling inadequate? Or scared? Or playful? She hoped it was the latter.

She laughed to lighten the mood, then he reached out and pulled her into his arms, against his rock-hard chest. His mouth descended on hers. A searching, gentle kiss that sent spasms of need all the way to her toes. He expertly drew her in and made her want so much more. He raised his head and she gasped for breath.

Then he released her, and she stepped away and turned down the bed, leaving the top sheet where they could grab it if they wanted. She had her own qualms about getting naked with him. But not enough to stop her. She knew what she wanted.

He sat on the edge of the bed and took off his shoes. She sat beside him and took hers off too. Then her jacket, belt, and holster. Then the rest of her clothes until she was naked beside him. He watched her and the heat of his gaze scorched her skin. She put her clothes on the other bed and he pulled off his shirt.

He took a small packet out of his pants pocket. He'd come prepared. Something she hadn't thought about. She took his clothes as he handed them to her and put them on the other bed. They needed to look neat when they got back to the house.

When he was down to nothing but briefs, all she could see was the big bulge waiting for her. He pulled off the briefs and she looked at him. How would it feel with him inside her? Her body clenched. She'd soon find out.

She crawled onto the bed and he followed her. They lay side by side and he folded her into his arms and kissed her again, long and hard and wet. She couldn't get enough.

"It's been a long time," Doug said quietly. "Let's take it slow and easy and see what develops."

He was as unsure as she was. That helped. "We don't have to hurry. That cop can wait." She snuggled closer.

He started an expert exploration of her body, hands and tongue moving from her neck to her breasts, then lower. He caressed her upper arm where the scar from her surgery had torn a jagged line downward.

When she didn't think she could wait any longer, he kissed her again, deeply, then sheathed himself and pushed into her center. Side by side on the bed. Gently probing until he filled her. She couldn't help but start moving. She arched against him, the friction building as he stroked deeply, in and out. Not a desperate building, but a gentle nudge of delight. He made her feel whole again. No pain. No fear. Gentle strokes of rapture. Building. Building. Until she rode the heights of completion, pure contentment as she convulsed around him. He let her settle against him, then drove into her again, thrusting again and again until he exploded inside her, sending new waves through her. She shuddered and he pulled her tight and held on to her, his breathing rasping and rapid.

"Wow." Pleasure sparked through her. That's all he said. But it was enough.

He kissed her again. Long and deep and magical. His hands caressed her breasts, her shoulders, her back. Then he pulled back and looked at her body. At her scars. His eyes darkened.

"Kenny did that?" He traced the thin line down her left breast.

"He liked to make me bleed. I swear it turned him on."

"I'm glad you shot him."

"So am I. He can't hurt anyone else, ever again."

He traced the line that ran down her chest, between her breasts, all the way to her navel. "He was sadistic. Must have been psychotic."

"None of that showed at first. Only later, after he had me completely in his power. I'll never let another man have that kind of power over me again."

"I wouldn't want that kind of power over a woman." Doug's voice held sincerity.

She believed him. But could she trust him with her heart? It could be damaged, even more than her body.

A tiny bit of panic crept in. "We'd better get back to the house. They'll be sending a search party out after us."

He laughed. "And won't they be surprised?" He sat up.

She gazed at his legs. At the scars that snaked down both shins. And the scars on his right thigh. "You're lucky to be walking."

"The doctor wanted to take off the right leg. I told him no. To patch me up the best he could. And he did."

"And you're walking enough to keep some muscle tone."

"I can't run. I can't crawl around in tight places. I can't defend myself in a fight."

"You have us to help you."

"I guess you know I'm counting on you if it comes down to the fight." His expression sobered. "Now we have to get back to work. Back to the real world." He glanced back at the tousled bed. "We have a fight to finish, then we can think about the future."

Her spirits plummeted. There wouldn't be any more stolen moments until Moreno was in jail. Or dead.

CHAPTER 22

*D*oug drove out of the parking lot, making sure the unmarked car was following. "We have our escort, but keep your eyes open anyway. Just in case he misses something."

He glanced at Alison. She was quietly watching the traffic around them. Not saying anything. Was she sorry they'd made love? He'd been so diligent to keep their relationship strictly professional that he hardly knew her. They didn't often engage in small talk. Now he felt tongue-tied and awkward around her. He wanted to touch her, but was afraid to. Damn.

"We just passed one suspicious car." She turned back to look. "It's sitting at the side of the road and not moving."

"What color? What is it?"

"An old gray Mustang. Dull paint, dirty. Two Hispanics inside." Her tone was all business.

Because of the danger, it had to be that way. But he'd felt her withdrawing as soon as they'd left the hotel room. He took a deep breath and focused on his driving. And getting back to the house quickly.

As soon as he pulled into the driveway, their escort vehicle sped away.

Once inside the house, Alison headed up the stairs without a word. He watched her go and wondered how wrong he could have been. They needed to talk. But he also needed to keep his mind on the problems at hand. Before he got them all killed.

Scott came down the stairs, two at a time. "A dirty gray car stopped, looked at the house, then sped off to the west."

"Damn. That car was not following us. Alison saw it at the side of the road."

Dave stuck his head out of the den. "I'll go check your car for a GPS. My specialty." The back door banged shut behind him. He was back within five minutes. "Right under the bumper." He held it up "I'll take this baby for a ride, so they think Doug has left again." He grabbed his jacket and helmet from the chair in the living room, then went back outside.

Doug heard the motorcycle spin out of the driveway and head east. That might fool Moreno and his boys for a few minutes, but doubted they'd believe it for long. He went in search of Alison.

And found her sitting in her bedroom, the door open, checking her revolver.

"I heard Dave say something about a GPS. That gray Mustang."

"Yeah. Scott saw it out front. Are you ready to go through another attack?" What an inane thing to say to her. But it was what popped out of his mouth. Not lover talk. Agency talk. For now.

"We could leave." She looked at him and said it without conviction in her voice.

"No we can't. I should say, I can't. You can. If you want to go, go without guilt. I don't blame you at all for wanting to leave."

She set down the gun and stood. "I'll stay and take my chances, again. They will attack. Maybe something different this time, since their firepower hasn't worked so far."

"That's what I'm afraid of."

"Where did Dave go? I heard his bike leave."

"He took the GPS to ditch it somewhere."

"Damn. I wish we'd thought about a GPS. They had plenty of time to conceal it."

A pang of guilt hit him. All that time in the room upstairs. "Let's go downstairs, to the den. We need to stay there as much as possible."

She put her gun in its holster on her belt and picked up her laptop.

Doug stopped at Scott's room and stuck his head in. "Still quiet out there?"

"No signs of any hostiles yet." Scott grinned at them.

"You can join us in the safe room. With that screen removed and the window open, they can see you. You don't have to stay here and be a target."

"I'll stay on watch. Sound the alarm."

"Be careful." He didn't like leaving Scott so exposed. Their safe house was no longer safe.

No one was in the den when Alison followed Doug inside. He turned and reached for her hand and pulled her close. "Did I make a mistake?"

He caught her by surprise. She'd thought he'd had second thoughts. Like she had. She settled against him. "No. I guess I'm

176

running scared. I don't know. Let's wait until everything is resolved. When Moreno is out of the picture. Then see what happens." She said it quietly, not wanting anyone to overhear. She wasn't sure how others in the agency would take a liaison between the boss and one of the employees.

"We can do that." He gave her a quick kiss, not lingering and seeking. An affirmation. A promise. Then he smiled, that sweet smile she'd seen lately when he wasn't troubled.

She'd deal with the ramifications later of a relationship with the boss. "You do realize Moreno won't wait. He'll strike today and hard."

"I was trying to forget it for a minute." That sweet smile again. Then his expression sobered.

The back door banged open and she tensed. Doug did too, then released his hold on her. She stepped back, waiting.

"Just me," Rafe called from the kitchen. "I brought take and bake pizzas for dinner tonight."

Rafe appeared at the door to the den. "I'll pop them in the oven when we're ready for them."

"Good thinking," Doug said.

"I'll go take the watch at the back window upstairs." The back door opened again. "Jake and Erik were outside." Rafe left. His footsteps pounded on the stairs.

Erik and Jake came into the room. "We walked as much of the perimeter as we could," Jake said. "That side gate is the only fast way in. I chained it shut and added a padlock. They'll have to bust it down to come in that way with a vehicle."

"They could come over the top, like commandos," Alison said. "On foot."

"That's true. If they plan a stealth approach instead of hitting with tons of firepower, like they did at Dave's. Anything else we need to do?" Doug asked.

"Pray?" Alison said it as half jest, but half serious too. She didn't want to go through a third siege, but had to find the courage to stay. Even if Doug had other help, she couldn't abandon him. He meant too much to her, despite her reservations about a future with him.

"Judging from Moreno's past hits," Jake said, "my guess is we get bullets first. Then they might come back with fire, to make sure."

"Have they done that in Los Angeles?" Alison asked. "Bullets and fire?"

"Several times I know of." Jake pushed the door closed. "Time to get ready. They may not wait until dark. Strike first and fast is their motto."

"Uh, Jake. Thanks for sticking around today." Doug said the words sincerely.

"I'm agency now. I don't like how Hensley is treating you." Jake sat in the chair by the window.

Erik booted his computer. "I'll lose myself in database checking so I won't panic." He laughed at himself.

Alison watched from behind his chair. Doug took the left end of the couch and rested his right leg on the cushions. She could tell he was hurting, but knew he wouldn't admit it if she asked.

Her private cell phone buzzed in her left pocket. She jumped and pulled it out. "The woman from the Harney house, Mariana Perez." She answered.

"Armando say his father going to attack again," she said in her accented English. "He knows where you are."

"Thanks for telling us," Alison said. "Are you okay? Not in any danger?"

"We were told to get our things ready to move fast if something happens. They didn't say what."

"You stay safe. I hope we can help you when this is over."

"I hope so too. Moreno plans to kill as many as he can. Watch for men with assault rifles. They've left the house in the hills."

"Do you have any idea what area the house is in?"

"No. Only Armando knows."

"Okay. We're getting ready," Alison said.

"I have to go. Stay safe." Marianna ended the call.

Alison relayed the messages to the rest of the group.

"We're as ready here as we can be." Doug sat up and picked up his phone. "I'm calling Chet now and demanding SERT coverage." He held the phone, listening. "Voice mail." He waited. "Chet. Call me immediately. I need SERT now. Moreno's boys are on their way to Jake's."

"I'll go check to see if Scott needs a break from the window." Jake left the room.

His heavy steps on the stairs echoed through the house.

Panic seized Alison, cutting off her breath. She leaned against the paneling, trying to force breaths past the blockage in her chest. Her heart rate accelerated until she thought it would break out of her chest.

Doug saw her distress and levered himself off the couch, enveloping her in a crushing hug.

"Take it easy. We'll get through this."

She leaned into his strength.

CHAPTER 23

*D*oug held Alison against his chest and felt her rapid heartbeat. "Calm down, easy, breathe deeply." Her panic scared him more than the prospect of an attack.

She took a ragged breath, then another.

Erik had stopped working and stared at them.

He eased her over to the couch. "Sit." She sank down on the cushions. And he sat next to her, pulling her into his arms again. "Relax against me. Let me hold you."

Some of the tenseness seemed to leave her body. She was breathing, though raggedly.

She glanced toward Erik, then pulled out of his arms, as if realizing what was happening. "I'm okay now. Just a flashback. Jake's heavy footsteps on the stairs. Like Kenny when he was coming after me."

"Not the attack that's coming? Are you sure?"

"Well, maybe some of it. But not all. I'll be all right. I prom-ise. I won't let you down."

"I know you won't. Hey, I'm sorry about the memories."

Jake opened the door and came in. "Scott's okay with staying on watch. Not that it will do us much good."

"If he stays back, he'll be safe there." Doug's phone rang. He picked it up. "Chet." He answered.

"What's this about shooters on the way? How do you know?"

"Moreno's boys found the house. They put a GPS on the car at the hotel."

"You're sure?"

"Dave is taking the GPS for a ride, but Alison got a call from the woman at the Harney Street house that shooters have left the country hideout and are heading our way."

"That's good enough for me. I'll send SERT immediately and deal with any fallout later. Be careful." He ended the call.

Doug set down the phone. "Now we wait to see if SERT gets here before Moreno's boys."

Alison stood. "We know they're coming. Scott and Rafe need to be in here too. She started for the door."

The roar of the cars came first, then the burst of automatic rifle fire. "They're here." Panic laced her words.

Gut-wrenching spasms hit Doug. "Sounds like two vehicles." He dropped to the floor. Erik and Alison hit the floor too. Jake moved toward the window. The escape hatch. Doug reached out and grabbed Alison's hand and held on. She was lying near, with her eyes shut, rigid and unmoving.

Windows shattered. Bullets hit the wall but didn't penetrate the bulletproofing. The sound of the pings grated on his ears.

Then the shooting stopped.

Sirens. The cars raced away.

"SERT should have been here sooner." He didn't want anyone hurt. This was his fight.

"Scott's hit." Rafe called down the stairs.

Doug got up from the floor and pulled Alison to her feet.

"I'll go check on Scott." Jake opened the den door and ran up the stairs.

Doug picked up his phone and called 911, requesting an ambulance. He moved carefully into the hallway, dodging the debris on the floor. Then limped up the stairs, Alison behind him.

Scott was sprawled on the floor and Jake was using a T-shirt to apply pressure to his upper arm. Scott was moaning and thrashing his legs. Alison went to his head and steadied him, cradling his head in her lap.

"Help is on the way," Doug said. "Hang on, buddy."

"I...got...one," Scott said. "Then they fired back. Two cars."

"Don't talk. Save your strength," Doug said. "You took too big a chance. You could have been killed."

Another siren, the ambulance. The paramedics rushed up the stairs and took over stabilizing Scott. Doug and Alison moved out of the way and headed back downstairs. Several police cars had arrived with SERT and the officers were waiting for them.

"Two patrol cars are in pursuit." The officer glanced up the stairs. "Someone was hit?"

"Yeah. One man down, though still alive," Doug said. "We could have used help sooner."

"We weren't authorized to stay in place."

"I know. We've already caused the death of two police officers."

"Moreno and his gang caused the death of those two, not you. Chet said to remind you of that."

Doug limped around the downstairs with two officers, assessing the damage. Most of the shots hit the living room and dining room. Their attack was cut short.

The paramedics came down with Scott on a gurney. Jake

and Rafe followed.

"Where are you taking him?" Doug asked.

"OHSU, the trauma center there," one replied.

"I'll go with him," Erik said. "And stay until we know he's okay."

"Good idea," Doug said. "Stick with him. You'll be safe there too."

He gazed down at Scott. "We're with you, buddy. Take care." The paramedics wheeled him out and the ambulance took off.

Alison pushed off from the wall where she'd been leaning. "Another house shot up. For what?"

"I can't tell Moreno I'll meet him one on one," Doug said.

"I didn't mean that." She shook her head. "I meant why is he so determined to destroy as much as he can?"

"Because that's his nature. He's an evil man and determined to get revenge at all costs."

She frowned. "I'm confused, upset, scared."

"We all are. Come here."

She walked into his arms and let him hold her. And the tears started. He heard her sniffling as she tried to keep them back.

"Go ahead and cry. Release some of that tension." He held her closer and stroked her back. And listened to her cry. That's all he could do to help.

He shifted his weight and she pulled away. "I'm sorry. I shouldn't have leaned on you." She headed for the den.

He let her go. He had to stay accessible to the officers in charge.

Jake and Rafe milled around, looking at the damage. "I hope the DEA took out enough insurance," Jake said.

"I have an umbrella liability policy. But I hate seeing the damage to this lovely home."

Sirens left the house. Others arrived. Sirens wailed in the

distance. Doug wasn't sure which was worse, the waiting for the attack or the aftermath. Three major attacks, four if you counted the firebombing of his mother's house. His house didn't matter. Five days of utter mayhem.

Chet came in through what was left of the front door. "The patrol cars lost them. Both of them."

Doug stepped over the debris and joined him near what was left of the couch.

"First hint of a siren and they take off."

"How badly was Scott hit?"

"It's his upper left arm. And he's right handed. He should recover. He said there were two cars. And he hit one of the guys."

"Maybe he'll show up at an emergency room."

"If we get lucky."

"It's time you guys had a lucky break. It's been going all their way, so far. I'm going to look around."

"Not as much destruction as Dave's. They didn't have as much time." Doug stood in the middle of the room, unsure what he should be doing. Unsure what he could possibly do that would help.

Chet moved through the living room, checking the damage, then went upstairs.

Doug dropped down on a chair that hadn't been hit. Rafe sat on the edge of a partially destroyed couch. "Where's Dave? Did he come back?"

"He wasn't here during the attack and hasn't shown up. I hope they didn't spot him and take him out." Another worry. When would it end?

Chet came back downstairs and checked the other rooms on the lower floor. Then returned to the living room. "That safe room worked, anyway. No one hurt but Scott."

"Alison is thoroughly spooked." Doug glanced toward the den.

"She's sitting in there, staring at the wall," Chet said.

"I should have made her go to Hawaii."

Chet frowned, as if he'd thought of something. "She's a fighter. She'll survive."

"I'm worried about her." More worried about her than anyone else. He didn't like how that made him feel.

ALISON LEANED against the back of the couch, clutching a pillow to her chest. Looking for comfort where she could find it. Doug and Chet were in the living room talking, but she couldn't make out everything they were saying. They did mention her name several times. That she could pick up. She was miserable. She'd failed as a detective. She'd failed as a strong woman. She was nothing but a wimp.

Footsteps in the hallway and Doug's cane. He was coming and she wasn't ready to face him.

He stopped in the doorway. "May I join you?"

She could have sent him away, but that was postponing the inevitable. They would have to have this conversation eventually. Might as well be now.

"Come on in." She put down the pillow.

Doug sat on the other end of the couch and set his cane on the floor. "You're upset. We all are. Scott was shot. We were all in danger."

"I'm a coward. I was quaking with fear."

"That's not cowardice." He raised his voice a notch. "That's being human. Giving up is cowardice. You haven't given up. You've been through all three attacks. More than anyone else."

"That doesn't make it any easier."

"Of course not. It makes it harder. You've had plenty of time to be thoroughly scared. Like I said. That's being human." He inched closer to her.

"How can I go on? This isn't over. Moreno is still out there." She shuddered, letting her frustration show.

"One step at a time. Like I'm doing." Now his words were calm, even soothing.

"Moreno could send more cars, more men with assault rifles. They could invade the house and shoot us all." She was being irrational and she knew it.

"Not now. The police are here."

"They won't stay all night." She glared at him. Beyond caring if she offended him. "And it all starts over again tomorrow."

"This safe room saved all of us who were in here."

She glanced around the room. At the lack of damage. At the panels that protected them. "Scott made this room secure, then he stayed upstairs."

"And made a mistake. Showing himself at the window."

"He said he hit someone."

"That didn't do him any good."

"You're right." She let out a big sigh. "We need to protect ourselves while we go after Moreno."

Doug smiled. "Now you're talking more positive." He scooted to the center of the couch.

"I'm a failure. I haven't done anything that helped."

"Yes, you have. You helped my mother escape the firebombing. You helped Dani when Dave's house was attacked. You drove me when I wasn't driving. And you've been right here beside me when I needed someone."

"I guess I've done my agency job." She looked at him. And a bigger smile than the other.

"That's right. Your job has not been to get Moreno. Your job is to support other people when they need help. That's what being a private investigator is all about."

"Will we ever get our lives back to normal? I want to go back to finding lost kids and investigating fraudulent insurance claims. Staking out cheating spouses."

This time he laughed. "Not boring at all, was it?"

"But you hired me because I was a good shot. And the only person I shot was Kenny, who was after me, not someone else."

"I hired you because I wanted you in the agency. I knew you'd be a good investigator. Besides, I wanted to get to know you better."

She stared at him. And it sunk in. He was telling her he valued her, not just her shooting.

"Come here." He motioned to her. She scooted closer, until she was next to him, her thigh touching his. He put his arm around her shoulders and pulled her close. Then kissed her, long and slow.

A different kind of kiss. One that seemed to promise more. Was she ready for more? When he released her, she pulled away, so they were no longer touching.

"What are you afraid of?" His voice was shaking.

Before she could form an answer, Chet appeared in the doorway. "Let's go grab a hamburger. Jake and Rafe are coming too. Then we can go up to the hospital to see Scott. I need a statement from him. By the time I get you back here, the crime scene people will be finished and the front door and windows will be boarded up."

What was she afraid of? Could she answer that question? They did need food and they needed to see Scott. They'd get back to their conversation later. Doug had that look in his eyes. He was one determined man.

CHAPTER 24

*D*oug's phone whistled to indicate an incoming text. He set down his hamburger and pulled out his phone. "Text from Dave. Good news." He kept his voice low because of the crowded fast food restaurant they were in. He read the message: "Followed the shooters. Located Moreno's hideout in the hills. Forest Grove area."

"Cross streets? Road?" Chet asked.

Doug typed a message and pushed send. And waited. "He must have come back to the house during the siege."

"And taken off after the cars," Chet said. "The first officer on the scene said he saw a motorcycle take off. Could have been Dave."

Another whistle. Doug read the words aloud: "Gotta go. Hostiles."

"Hills? Forest Grove?" Jake set down his drink. "How much area are we talking about?"

Doug glanced at his phone. Willing it to produce another

message. "Large area. Woods. Vineyards. Farms. We need more information." He picked up his hamburger.

His phone rang. Erik.

"Scott's in surgery. He's stable and should be okay." Erik sounded relieved.

"We're grabbing a hamburger, then heading for the hospital."

"Bring me a hamburger. I hate hospital food."

Doug relayed the message and Chet went to the counter to order the burger for Erik.

He returned to the table. "The department owes you a lot more than hamburgers and fries. For being bait for the DEA." He looked at Jake and smiled.

"Hensley would deny that," Jake said. "But it's the truth. Which is why I've thrown in with the agency. And Will Siegel too."

Alison was quiet, withdrawn. She was returning to her old self, that guarded self that didn't let anyone in. Just when he thought he was making progress with her, she ran scared, back to her defensive position. With Moreno still out there, the future was murky.

They finished eating and Rafe dumped their trash while Chet picked up the order for Erik. Then they headed for the hospital.

Erik grabbed for the sack in Chet's hand. "Just in time. I was starving. Anything happening?" He pulled out the hamburger and took a big bite.

Another whistle. "Dave found the hideout. Here's another message." Doug read it aloud. "No sign on the road to the house. Turned right off of Gales Creek Road, back in the hills on a narrow road."

Doug asked him where he was now. And read the return

message: "Hiding in the woods. Hid my bike out near the road under a huge oak tree. Hiked in."

"What's he planning to do?" Chet asked.

Doug typed the question.

The answer: "They posted guards below me. Eight men between me and the road. I'm stuck."

"Oh, hell." Rafe said.

"Tell him to keep his cell phone on and we'll triangulate and find him," Chet said. He called the precinct and relayed the problem and Dave's cell number. "Now we wait."

"I've got to let Hensley know what's going on." Jake made a call and updated the DEA. "We'll get full cooperation and a hostage bargaining team if we need one."

"If we need one." Doug snickered. "That's a joke. Of course we need one. We're not storming in there to rescue Dave and find Moreno all by ourselves."

"Don't even think about it," Chet said. "Dave's okay for now."

He sent Dave another text: "Sit tight. We're working on it."

Doug's stress level was as high as it could go. "Scott's in surgery, Dave's in danger, and I'm sitting in a hospital waiting room, completely helpless." He said the words quietly, to no one in particular.

Alison reached out and took his hand. Surprising him. His business as a private investigator was on the line. As well as the lives of his people and his own life.

"We'll get him out," she said. "Dave's a resourceful guy. Trust him. Trust all of us."

Another text from Dave: "Moving away from the perimeter guards. Toward the house. Safer."

Nick came in the door. "I got Chet's message that you were coming here. How's Scott?"

"In surgery," Doug said.

Nick sat in a chair and settled down to get comfortable. "Anything else happening?" He was looking at Doug's phone in his hand.

"I'm getting texts from Dave. He found Moreno's hideout in the woods."

"That's good news." Nick's back straightened. And a half smile shown on his face.

"But he's stuck. Armed guards he can't get past. Now we have to find him."

"So, what are you doing sitting here?" Nick's tone was sarcastic.

If it was an attempt at humor, it fell flat. Doug wanted to be out there hunting for Dave and the hideout.

"I won't let them go charging up there to get themselves killed," Chet said.

"I could go by myself," Rafe said. "Find his bike and pinpoint what road it is, for the assault later."

"What assault?" Chet asked. "There will be no armed assault on the house. A team will go in and get them to surrender."

"You can't go. It's Forest Grove," Alison said. "Out of your jurisdiction."

"But not DEA jurisdiction. However, we're not authorized to launch an assault either," Jake said. "Our goal is collecting evidence."

"These men have committed crimes. It's no longer a simple court case involving drug running," Doug said. "They've killed and wounded and shot up property."

"And gotten away with it," Alison said. "Nothing is being done. And Dave is risking his life now while we sit here." She got up and paced the floor. "There must be something we can do."

Chet stood. "I'm going to notify the Washington County

Sheriff, the State Police, and the FBI. They all have jurisdiction. Those guys out there are cop killers." He went out into the hallway to make his calls.

Chet returned about ten minutes later and sat down. "Deputies on patrol in the countryside will be looking for anything unusual and looking for Dave's bike under that oak tree. And they will add more patrols. State police and FBI are on standby."

Doug shifted on the uncomfortable chair. "A long shot, finding that bike. They need to locate his phone."

A doctor appeared at the door. "Scott came through surgery just fine. He's in recovery. When he's moved to a room, he can have two visitors at a time." He turned and left.

Doug's phone whistled again. This time it was a picture. Two men on a deck, sitting with beers in their hands. Ramon Moreno and Armando Moreno. No mistaking the two of them.

"Here's the proof we needed. Moreno is there." He passed the phone around.

"Now what do we do?" Alison asked. "They're killers. Someone needs to go in after them."

"We do nothing now," Chet said. "We wait for agencies with jurisdiction."

Jake stood. "I need to go see Hensley. This is the proof we needed."

"Take me with you." Rafe looked sharply at Doug. A message. He wasn't waiting.

"Do you need a ride back to your cars?" Nick asked. "I can take you. I have a witness I need to track down tonight."

"I'm forwarding the picture to your cell phone," Doug said.

"Thanks." Jake nodded.

The three men left the waiting room. No more waiting impatiently.

∽

"ARE we going to be safe at the house tonight?" Alison wasn't sure she wanted to go back to Jake's. But that was where Chet was taking them.

"I'll get you at least one patrol car on watch. Two if I can." Chet pulled into the driveway and around back.

"I've tried three more times to send a message to Dave," Doug said. "His phone quit working."

"His signal was weakening," Chet said. "I got a call that the triangulation didn't work."

"I hope that's all it is," Doug said. "I have a bad feeling. I don't like him out there alone all night."

They went inside and Chet called dispatch and was told he'd get one patrol car for the night.

"You don't want us to leave, I guess," Doug said.

"I definitely don't want you to leave," Chet said. "Stay here and get some sleep. Tomorrow we deal with Dave's situation when we have daylight to find the road and him." He scowled. "As members of the task force, Nick and I can go out there. We'll keep you informed of Dave's situation. But you stay far away from that place." His tone was demanding.

Alison went into the living room. The front door and windows had been covered with plywood. But nothing had been done to clean up the damage inside the house. Tomorrow was soon enough. Exhaustion warred with the desire to stay awake, on watch. Sleep might win tonight.

She returned to the dining room. Doug was sitting at the table. At least the table escaped the barrage of gunfire.

Erik went up the stairs.

"I mean it, Doug," Chet said. "Stay here. You'll be safe here tonight. They don't yet know how much damage they've done or who got shot."

"How do you know what they know?" Alison didn't try to hide her natural cynicism. Moreno's gang always knew more than they realized.

"We don't, for sure. An educated guess."

"And if you're wrong?" Doug asked.

"I'm leaving an armed guard for you, outside."

"One car, one cop. I'm not feeling very secure." Alison's deep rumble of intuition told her it wasn't enough. Yet what could she do. Doug was tired and needed sleep. So did she.

"I'll tell the other patrols to do a frequent drive-by. Keep your phones handy." Chet left through the back door.

Erik came back down. "I was going to offer to watch out that front window, but it's boarded up too."

"You need your sleep. We all do." Doug stood. "Go to bed."

Erik headed up the stairs.

Doug leaned on his cane, walked several steps.

"You're wobbly on your feet. Let's go upstairs. Or do you want to stay down here in the den tonight?" She watched the play of emotion on his face.

"I need to stretch out and relax, whether I sleep or not."

"Sleep is what you need. And so do I."

She followed him up the stairs. Slowly. He pulled himself by his left hand and balanced with his cane.

At the top of the stairs, he turned to her. "We should stay together tonight. Fully dressed and ready for whatever might happen."

"Good idea. And I'm going to add a little more to my outfit." She went into her room and Doug followed. She pulled open her shirt, revealing an undershirt underneath. She took a small revolver out of her bag and put it into the mini holster built into the undershirt, under her left arm. Then she added a small knife to a slim pocket under the holster.

Doug watched her without comment. He knew she needed the extra insurance and reassurance. He understood her. And that's what made him special for her.

He sat on the edge of the bed and took off his shoes, then got comfortable on the back side, letting her have the front side. She kicked off her shoes, turned off the lamp, and settled onto her back, staring up at the dark ceiling. As keyed up as she was, sleep was not going to be easy, though she was bone tired.

And feeling strange. Sharing a bed with Doug. Like they were old friends, or lovers. Or just because. Then she realized that she felt uncomfortable because nothing was clear about their relationship. They'd made love. They'd been through terrifying attacks. They'd managed to survive. That had forged the bond that existed.

But something else. She loved him. Deeply, passionately. But would they survive and be able to build a life together?

CHAPTER 25

*D*oug woke with a start. He sat up in the bed and listened. Nothing. Had he heard something? Or was his imagination playing tricks on him? Alison was breathing softly at his side. Still asleep.

He rolled over and tried to go back to sleep. And stared, unseeing, into the darkness.

Rafe wasn't here. That was the problem. Rafe was the one who checked the downstairs windows at night.

Doug had forgotten until now. He had to get up and check the windows for himself, then he could sleep.

He rolled to the side of the bed and stood. Then limped around to where he'd left his shoes, and used the chair in the room to sit and put them on. Still no sounds coming from downstairs. He'd check the windows, then come back to bed.

He picked up his shoulder holster and put it on. Picked up his Beretta from the nightstand and shoved it into the holster. Picked up his cane and a small mag light. He needed to get safely down the stairs in the dark.

He moved quietly into the hallway, and shut the bedroom door. When he reached the bottom of the stairs, he turned into the hallway, toward the back of the house, toward the rooms they weren't using, the rooms Rafe checked every night.

Three small rooms. The kind of rooms that became a private office, a kids' playroom, a sewing room. The window was locked tight in the first one. And the second one.

He opened the door to the last room, at the back corner of the house. And shone the light toward the window. It stood wide open. Before he had time to react, a sharp pain exploded on the back of his head. He slumped to the floor, his cane crashing down beside him. His world went black.

ALISON ROLLED over and reached out. Doug was gone. What had she heard? Her heart rate accelerated until it obliterated all other sounds. She patted the small holster under her arm. Her revolver was ready.

What woke her up? It sounded like a door closing. Could it have been the back door? She listened for any other sounds in the house. Something deep down inside her told her something was wrong. She felt it in her bones.

Slowly her body began to obey her commands to get out of bed. She slipped into her shoes. Still listening intently, she dug into her bag and found her small flashlight and turned it on. Doug's shoes and gun were gone. Maybe he'd heard something and went to investigate.

She went into the hall as Erik came from his bedroom. "Did you hear something?" she whispered.

"Yes. I'm going down," Erik said.

"You aren't armed."

"I hope you are. I'm just a geek."

"Stay behind me." She grabbed her revolver from its holster and led the way down the stairs. All she heard was the creak of the stairs.

Her light caught a trail of blood from the back of the house toward the kitchen. And her heart accelerated into overdrive. It was the back door she heard. "They've got Doug."

She pulled out her phone and called 911. Then crept down the hallway toward that last room, where the door stood open. The blood came from there. Erik followed her.

She peeked into the room. The window stood open. Doug's cane and empty holster were on the floor, along with a small pool of blood. She gasped and stepped back. Her heart pounded against her chest wall. "He's hurt. Or dead."

"They took him, so he's still alive," Erik said.

They followed the blood trail to the back door and outside. The blood led in the direction of the gate onto the side street. "They went out that way." She pointed.

"Where's the cop?" Erik asked.

They ran around the house to the driveway. A bullet had penetrated the back window. "He was shot from behind. He didn't have a chance." The officer was slumped over the steering wheel, part of his head blown away. Her stomach churned. She shuddered and averted her gaze.

"They don't care how many cops they kill," Erik said.

A siren blared in the distance.

Alison called Chet. "They kidnapped Doug. And killed another cop."

"Damn. I'm on my way. Did you call 911?"

"Yes. I hear the first unit coming."

"I'll be there as quickly as I can." He ended the call.

The early morning air was cool. Alison shivered. "I'm going

back inside." Erik followed her and they sat at the dining room table.

Her phone rang. It was Rafe.

"I hope it's not too early to call you. I found Dave's bike. And I saw an SUV drive out, with four men, about an hour ago."

"Those four men are probably the ones who just kidnapped Doug. And the cop in the driveway was shot and killed."

"Oh, shit. I should have called earlier. What should I do?"

"Chet's on his way here. I'll have him talk to you. I'm sure you need to stay there to watch for that SUV to come back and then direct any incoming DEA and sheriff units to the right road."

"I can do that. I have a good place to hide. Right where the bike was stashed."

Sirens grew louder and two patrol cars pulled into the driveway.

"We have company. Incoming units. I'll call you back with more information when I have it. Put your phone on vibrate." She ended the call.

She wanted to crawl off and cry for Doug, but she had to stay strong, face the questions, do whatever she could to help bring him back alive. That was the hope that would keep her going. That he was still alive and they could get him back.

DOUG MOANED. A sharp stab of pain hit him in his ribs. He managed to open his eyes a bare slit, enough to see Ramon Moreno standing over him. Kicking him. The next blow landed on his right leg and pain radiated through his entire leg and up his torso. He clenched his teeth to keep from crying out.

"Wake up. You're nothing but a helpless cripple."

He forced his eyes open and glared at Moreno. "So untie me and see how helpless I am." This was the closest he'd been to his arch enemy for years. Moreno had aged and grown flabby. "You're nothing but a vicious killer of unarmed young women." He smelled blood. Probably his own. But where?

"You killed my sons." He barked out the words.

"They were shooting at me. And two of my friends. Yes, I killed them. I'd do it again. If they were shooting at me."

Moreno stood directly over him, staring down. "And you destroyed my business in Los Angeles. Forced me to go to Mexico. I'll never forgive you for what you've done to me. You've been after me since I was young."

Doug tugged at the zip ties binding his wrists in front of him. His feet were also tied together. And dried blood congealed on the top part of his shirt. "You should have stayed out of the drug trade. You should have stayed away from my wife and daughters. You ran them out of Los Angeles."

"You were interfering with me. Drugs make my living. That's the way it's always been in my family. Americans buy our drugs. We make good money. You tried to destroy my business. And killed my sons. So I kill one daughter. And I kill the other when I find her."

"I hid her from you." He scowled at Moreno, though he wanted to choke the life out of him.

Moreno kicked him again in the ribs. The pain cascaded through him. He almost blacked out again. Fighting to stay awake, he rolled away from the blow. His head was pounding. A pool of thickened blood had been under his head. Then he remembered the flash of pain when he was hit.

"Come on. Get up, cripple. Fight me now."

"Untie me and I will."

Moreno laughed, that familiar cackle.

At least his hands were tied in front of him. That made it easier on his shoulders. He flicked his gaze around the small room, at the hardwood floor he lay on. No furniture in the room.

Alison wasn't there. Moreno hadn't gotten her too. Unless she was in another room. He hoped that whoever grabbed him hadn't gone upstairs. If he had to die, he didn't want her to die with him.

She could have been killed back at the house. And Erik. And that cop in the car. He willed away the thoughts and concentrated on his predicament. He was tied up in a room with his mortal enemy, Ramon Moreno. Why hadn't he killed him yet?

Armando Moreno burst into the room. He started talking in the Mexican dialect he grew up with. Doug knew enough of the language to follow what he said and what his father answered.

"Why is he here?" Armando asked. "Are you crazy? Diego said he killed the cop. That's three cops. Shooting up places. Now a kidnapping."

"Shut up. I'm running this organization. Not you."

"You're a fool. You'll have the police and the sheriff and the DEA down on us."

"They won't find us. We've been careful."

"You're going to die and I'm not going to be here. I want no part of your revenge against this man."

"You're a coward."

"I want to build the Oregon business, not go to jail for murder."

"After I finish with this bastard," he motioned toward Doug, "I'll concentrate on business."

"You'll be dead." Armando stormed out of the room and shouted to several men.

Moreno followed him into the hallway. "Send some men to the house to grab that blond bitch. I want her here."

"Are you going to kill her too?"

"After I let the men have her for sport. When she's ready to die, she dies. He watches her die. Then he dies, and I'm done. I've waited years for this day."

Doug's gut clenched, rock hard.

"You're crazy. I want no part of the killing. I'll have my men bring her here, but I'm not coming back and they aren't either. I'm taking my people to safety."

Moreno returned, looked in the door, then shut and locked it. Doug shifted on the floor, trying to get more comfortable. His head, his ribs, and his legs all ached.

He heard father and son arguing some more, but couldn't make out anything else they said. Then the front door opened and closed, and a vehicle sped away from the house.

CHAPTER 26

*A*lison choked down as much of her omelet as she could. Jake and Erik sat across from her in Doug's favorite diner. Doug had been gone for hours. He'd been bleeding when hustled out of the house. Was he hit? Stabbed? She hadn't heard a gunshot.

Erik set down his fork. "He could be dead by now. Why hasn't anyone gone in after him?"

"Vehicles are still going in and out that driveway," Jake said. "If the DEA is causing the delay, I'm resigning today."

Alison added cream to her coffee, to help her digest the coffee. Her stomach churned, but she needed the caffeine after so little sleep. "Could it be deliberate, to make Moreno think his hideout is still safe? So he won't kill Doug and run?"

"That's a possibility." Jake set down his coffee cup. "I did hear from Will about thirty minutes ago. Just before I got back to the house. Lots of activity at the house on Harney. He thinks they may be planning to leave."

The churning in her stomach intensified. "What's he seeing?"

"Stuff loaded into SUVs and a truck with a canopy. He also said one SUV took off with two men, carrying weapons."

Alison frowned. "I doubt they go anywhere without weapons. Will the DEA be in on the assault on the house? Will you be going?"

"Hensley is keeping me out of it and I don't know why. I'll go talk to him when I've finished breakfast. It could be a long day."

"They have to go in soon." She didn't disguise the pleading in her voice. "We have to keep hoping Doug is still alive." Her intuition told her he was. She didn't feel that he was gone.

They finished eating and went outside.

Erik unlocked his car and climbed in the driver's seat. "Are we going back to the house, Alison?"

"Nowhere else to go." She started around the car to the passenger side.

"I'll see you two later. I'm going downtown to see Hensley. I want to be in on the assault." Jake started across the lot toward his car.

A dark SUV careened into the lot and skidded to a stop. Both doors opened and two armed men jumped out.

Jake ran at the driver. He raised a pistol and fired. Blood oozed from a wound in his side, staining his shirt. He went down.

Alison screamed. The other man grabbed her and shoved her into the back seat of the SUV, climbing in after her. The driver got in and sped off.

"Okay, bitch. We got you." The man shoved her down on the seat and tied her wrists behind her with zip ties. He put a gag around her mouth and then tied her ankles together.

Her face pressed into the dirty seat cushion. The seat reeked of alcohol and cigarettes. She gagged. Nausea choked her. She was balanced precariously on the edge of the seat. The erratic driving of the man behind the wheel scared her as much as the prospect of seeing Moreno at the end of this wild ride.

When she started to slip off the seat, the man grabbed her arm, roughly, yanking her shoulder almost out of the socket. Pain radiated down her arm.

They hadn't searched her. She still had her revolver and knife. She lay still on the seat, not fighting, not wanting to call attention to herself. Maybe they wouldn't find the weapons. Her only hope was that Doug was still alive and she could somehow help him. Though that prospect looked doubtful. With her hands tied behind her, getting to her weapons was impossible.

HEAVY FOOTSTEPS SOUNDED in the hallway. Doug woke with a start. He'd been dosing, not getting the deep sleep he needed. He stirred, pain searing through his head, his ribs, his legs. He tried to roll to his side but was too weak. His ribs were on fire and his head throbbed.

The door opened and two men he'd never seen tossed Alison onto the floor, like she was a sack of feed.

She screamed around the gag in her mouth.

Rage roared through Doug. He could have killed those two men, if he could have gotten to them. The men glanced at him, then left, slamming the door.

"Hey. You okay?" A silly question. She was a captive too. Facing a far worse fate than he was.

Alison twisted around and her eyes widened. She maneuvered into a sitting position, despite the cords binding her hands behind her and binding her feet. And nodded her head.

She scooted toward him, then jerked her chin down and to the right. Several times.

"Your gun and knife?" He whispered the words. Hope kindled inside him.

She nodded again.

"Scoot closer. I'll see if I can get to them. Thank goodness my hands aren't tied behind me."

She leaned into him, as close as she could get to his hands.

"They could come at any time. Moreno is out there." He reached out and tugged at her blouse, getting both hands underneath and moving upward to the small pocket where the knife was hidden. He felt for the clasp and pulled out the knife. He maneuvered the knife from beneath her blouse and opened the blade.

She turned her back to him and he sliced at the ties on her wrists. The knife was sharp and cut through the plastic. When her hands were free, she pulled off the gag and took a deep breath. "They shot Jake. I don't know how bad. I didn't see where he was hit." She pulled her revolver from its holster and put it on the floor between them.

"Damn. Keep cutting. And we need to keep our voices at a whisper."

She cut his hands loose, then their feet.

He sat up, carefully. Dizziness whirled through him, and he fought to stay upright. Alison steadied him.

"Do you need to stay down?"

"Just a bit dizzy. I have a better chance sitting up."

"Let me see the back of your head." She looked at his wound. "It's not bleeding anymore. But it's going to need stitches. We have to get out of here." She went to the window and looked out. "Ten feet at least to the ground."

"Shh. Get on the floor. Someone could come." She obeyed,

moving close to him so their lack of bonds wouldn't be so obvious.

He tensed. Somewhere in the house people were running. Shouting. He caught a few words. "I think they found Dave. But they're also upset about something else."

"You can understand them?"

"Some of it."

"The hostage bargaining force is on its way," she said. "Maybe they're here. Rafe found the road."

"Good." Relief flooded through him. "Moreno's planned party won't happen."

"What do you mean?"

"He was going to bring his men in here and make me watch them rape you. Then kill you, then me."

She scooted closer to him and positioned her body so his hands were hidden, then put her hands behind her back. "That's why you're still alive."

"Yeah. Moreno wanted you too. He was angry when they only brought me in."

"Maybe I kept you alive in some small way."

"The thought of you being savaged by his men has given me hours of agony."

The door opened and Dave was roughly shoved into the room, his hands behind him. He stumbled. Then the door slammed and a key turned in the lock.

"Whoa! I didn't expect to see both of you here."

"I haven't been here long," Alison said.

"Why aren't you two tied up?"

"Shh. They didn't search me." She sat up and pulled out the knife. "Come here." He sat next to her and she cut his ties. "I have a revolver with five shots."

"Aim for Moreno," Doug said. "The rest of them are following him."

"I didn't see Armando. Is he still here?" Dave scooted away from them and leaned against the wall, his hands behind him.

"He left. He and Moreno argued and Armando said he's getting out so he can build the Oregon business. He expects his dad to die and the business will be his."

"That shows a little bit of intelligence," Alison said. "Moreno is blinded by his thirst for revenge."

"And we're still in a very tight spot." Doug shifted his position, to ease the aching in his ribs. "You two get over by the door. I'll stay on the floor. I can't do much in a fight anyway."

"We don't know how many will come in here," Alison said.

"I saw at least eight guards out along the driveway," Dave said. "There could be more men."

"Moreno will try to kill me before he'll give me up to negotiators." Doug scowled. He was sitting close to the big spot of his blood on the floor. Would Moreno come in shooting?

"I don't believe this conversation. I don't believe this week," Alison said. "It's unreal. This kind of mayhem doesn't happen to ordinary people minding their own business."

"He killed my daughter. That's what started this week's events."

"But you killed his two sons," Dave said. "So it started with you. Just playing Devil's Advocate here."

"He sent those two sons after me. It was me or them. But he doesn't see that. He was the one breaking the law. And his sons were breaking the law."

"Let's not argue." Alison got up from the floor. "Come on, Dave." She leaned against the wall behind where the door would open.

Doug saw her thinking. She'd be shielded and Moreno

wouldn't see the gun right away. Dave plastered himself against the wall on the other side of the door, where he could grab at whoever came in next.

Sounds came from outside. A bullhorn. The negotiating team was here, and far enough up the driveway they could see the house. Doug tensed. Anything could happen now. Moreno wouldn't give up without a fight, without trying to kill the three of them. They would be fighting for their lives.

"Are you sure you want to be a target down there?" Dave said.

"No. I need to be against that wall too." He attempted to get up, but his legs wouldn't cooperate.

Dave helped him up and over to where Alison was standing. Doug leaned against the wall to her right, then Dave returned to his spot on the other side of the door.

"Are you still dizzy?" Alison asked. "Stay against the wall. I'm keeping my hands free to act quickly."

"Don't worry about me. Defend yourself." Doug listened. "I haven't heard any shots. The response team must have rounded up the guards without a fight."

"How many men are in the house now?" Alison asked. "Do we have any idea?"

"I saw four," Dave said. "Including Moreno."

"Someone's coming." Doug flattened himself against the wall, tensed and ready.

Alison clicked the safety off her revolver.

CHAPTER 27

*D*oug strained to hear the voices in the hallway and identified three different ones. "Three armed men coming." He kept his voice to a whisper. Alison had five shots.

The key turned in the lock and the door banged open. Hitting Alison. Her gun dropped to the floor and she slid down the wall to the floor. Doug dove onto the gun and rolled away, turning onto his back. He still had his upper body strength, even though his legs weren't as strong as they used to be.

Moreno fired wildly, several shots at the place where Doug had been on the floor. He'd planned a quick kill that didn't work. When his eyes registered that Doug wasn't there, he glanced right, then left.

Doug fired one shot at Moreno's chest and he twisted around, still on his feet. Doug fired a second shot at his chest and he went down, his gun clattering to the floor. The two other men came through the door, firing wildly. Dave knocked the rifle out of the hand of one of the men.

Doug winged the other in his shooting arm and his rifle

dropped to the floor. Alison grabbed Moreno's gun and aimed it at the man who hadn't been shot.

He put up his hands. "Don't shoot."

The other man grabbed his wounded arm, to stem the flow of blood.

"Over there." Alison pointed to the far wall. The two men moved to where she said.

Doug checked Moreno for a pulse. It was weak. He was still alive. Doug scooted away from him. "Dave, take a gun and check the rest of the house. I thought there was another man inside."

"I'll try to signal the guys outside too." Dave left the room.

Moreno was unconscious and slipping away, blood flowing from two wounds in his chest. Relief flooded through Doug. He hated having to kill someone, but Moreno was an animal, sub human.

Dave came back with a young man, his hands above his head. He joined the others against the wall. Alison had grabbed an assault rifle from the floor and no one moved.

"Now see if you can alert the team outside without getting shot." Doug tried to get up from the floor, but fell back down.

"Stay put," Alison said. "Help will get here soon enough."

"I'll wave a white flag." Dave pulled a handkerchief out of his pocket.

"Moreno is gone." Doug let the relief flow through him. "I saw his last gasp of breath."

"Good," Alison said. "One less problem for the police. DEA will have to take down his organization another way."

Officers with assault rifles were the first inside the door. They secured the house and escorted Moreno's men outside. Two officers helped Doug to his feet and supported him out to the front and down the steps. An ambulance drove into the yard and the medics examined the gash on his head and told him he needed stitches at the emergency room.

"I'm not going to argue with you. I still feel woozy." The medics brought out a gurney and he laid down on it. The pounding in his head had intensified with all the movement.

The medics checked the bullet wound in the arm of the other man who was shot and wrapped it up. Two officers put him into a patrol car and took him away.

Chet and Nick ran up the road. Chet leaned over the gurney. "Were you shot?"

"No. The wound on my head needs stitches."

"Is Moreno dead?"

"Doug shot him," Alison said. "He saved us."

"So that's why everyone out here on guard duty gave up without firing a shot," Chet said. "They knew Moreno was going to die. He was acting crazy, they said."

"Armando had already deserted him, taking some of the men with him," Alison said.

"That's good news and bad news," Chet said. "We'll still have to deal with him in the future."

"Is it okay if I go to the hospital with Doug?" Alison asked.

"No, we need your statement and Dave's," Chet said. "The crime scene people are going to want to know what happened in there. Nick can go with Doug and get his statement after he gets stitched up."

The gurney was lifted into the ambulance and Nick climbed in behind it. Doug glanced at the wistful look on Alison's face as the door closed. What was that all about? He desperately needed to talk to her, and soon. He had a feeling all was not right yet between them.

～

ALISON STOOD STILL as the ambulance headed down the driveway. She should be with him.

Chet approached her. "He'll be all right. Let's go down to my car."

"I know he'll be all right. He's the strongest man I've ever known." She followed Chet down the driveway, to where his patrol car was parked along the side.

"Get in the front passenger seat and I'll use my computer to take down your statement. Save some time that way."

She opened the passenger door and got in. Chet settled into the driver's seat and positioned his computer keyboard so he could type.

Instead of the questions she expected, Chet stared at her. "I'm going to say something that may out of line. But I have to ask. You're not going to let Doug down, are you?"

"Are you playing matchmaker?"

"You two belong together."

Chet had surprised her. "I don't know. So much has happened."

His gaze was intense. "Give it some time."

"I do need time." She had a sudden thought. "Is Jake alive?" She blurted out the question.

"Yes. He was in surgery last I heard. Took a bullet in his left side. I'll find out how he is and let you know."

"Thanks. He tried to stop those guys from taking me. He did come through when the bullets started flying. But got in the way of that bullet."

"It's serious. But he's young and strong."

"Those men who grabbed me. Armando's men. They didn't search me. I had my revolver and a knife."

Chet opened a file on his laptop and started a recorder, giving his name, her name, date and time, and the circumstances. "Okay, talk me through everything that happened from the time you walked out of that diner."

She took a deep breath and began her narrative.

Several times Chet stopped her for clarification of a fact, but mostly he wrote down what she was saying. When he had finished, he gazed at her. "Moreno may be dead, but he was a fool. Armando could be a tougher gang leader to bring down. The DEA will have to start all over, building their case against him."

"He'll start selling drugs in Oregon and build up his own gang. That seemed to be his intention all along, according to what Doug overheard Moreno and Armando arguing about."

"We'll have to keep an eye on Harney Street."

"If they stay there."

"If they're smart, they won't," Chet said. "They must know by now that we've located that house."

"I hope they don't know that Mariana has called me several times."

"Let me know if she calls again. Maybe we can help her get away from him and back to where she wants to be."

"That's what she's hoping for, help getting away." She hesitated. "I need to get away." The urge to run was building inside her the whole time she talked through the details of the morning.

"You're exhausted by these days of dodging bullets. Like I said, give it time."

"I have a former foster mother in the little town of Exeter in the central valley in California. I may go there to get my bearings."

He shook his head. "Don't run. Stay and work things through, with Doug. He's hurting too and needs you. You'll both be stronger for it."

"And you're an expert?" Her irritation rose.

"I'll tell you my story someday. From my patrol days. From my first marriage. From the biggest mistake I ever made." His eyes bore into hers. "Don't make a rash decision you'll regret later."

"Committing to Doug would be a rash decision."

He smiled. "I don't think so. Nick and I planned that lunch meeting carefully. The location."

She felt the heat rise in her cheeks.

He smiled again. "Just saying. Don't throw away what you've already built between you. You two belong together."

"I don't know."

"Don't rush your decision, on anything. Stick around. See if you can heal here. You have friends who will help, who've been through it too."

She gazed at the older man, so wise and a good detective. Something to think about later.

CHAPTER 28

*D*oug leaned on Nick's arm and stumbled up the back steps and into the kitchen. His head spun, like it wasn't attached to his shoulders. Images in front of him drew closer, then further away. The pounding in his head increased. Normal for a concussion, the doctor had said. And this was a mild concussion.

"You could have stayed in the hospital overnight," Nick said quietly.

"No. I couldn't. I need to be here." Doug mumbled the words.

"You're still as stubborn as you've ever been."

Doug glared at him, then tried to balance on his weak legs but couldn't. Nick steadied him, and kept him from falling. Kept him from embarrassing himself in front of Alison. "Thanks."

The expression on Alison's face as she rushed to his side, was one of horror. He obviously looked like he felt, a mess. A white bandage was wrapped around his head, and his bloody shirt had been replaced by a shorty hospital gown. At least he still had his pants on.

Dave peeked in the kitchen door. "I'll grab you a shirt from the bedroom." He headed for the stairs.

"Let's get you to a chair or a couch," Nick said.

Alison reached for his free arm and helped support him out of the kitchen.

"A chair. I'm hungry. Do I smell pizza?"

"Yes. We're all hungry." Rafe had followed them as far as the kitchen door. "The pizzas I brought in yesterday are in the oven. And a salad in the refrigerator. I'll have them on the table in ten minutes."

"We'll get out of the way." Alison helped Nick get Doug to the dining room.

He sank onto the chair by the window. The sudden movement sent a stab of pain ricocheting through his ribs. "Thanks. I'm weak."

"You lost a lot of blood." Nick sat next to him. "And if you don't mind, I'll stay for pizza. I'm hungry too."

"I'm sure there's plenty. And thanks for all you've done for me today."

Dave appeared with a shirt that buttoned, so no need to put it on over the bandage. That helped.

Alison sat in a chair at the side of the table, not close to him. "And you need sleep."

"I know. Later." She was too far away. Keeping her distance, as she had for years. He craved a reassurance they could build on what had happened between them these last few days. Before he'd be able to sleep. But he had something else to do too. "After we eat, I'm calling Dani and my mother. I need my phone and my cane."

Alison stood. "I'll get them."

"Bring me the cane with the eagle head. It's in my closet."
Maybe the cane from Apache Joe would help. He needed something to give him strength and courage for the rest of the
evening. The eagle symbolizes courage, according to
Apache Joe.

Alison glanced back at him with a puzzled expression, then
headed for the stairs.

After he'd eaten, he'd do his best to get some alone time with
Alison. They needed to talk before she ran scared. After all
she'd been through, he couldn't blame her. Somehow he had to
change her mind and keep her with him.

Alison returned with his phone and the eagle head cane. "Sit
here." He patted the chair next to him. "And thanks."

She stood the cane against the wall behind his chair and
handed him the phone. He detected a moment's hesitation, then
she sat. Still too much distance between them. But it would
have to do for now.

"We're all still in shock. I need to get back to running the
agency, not facing death every day."

"Can we go back to the way things were?" Her voice carried
a plaintive tone.

He wished he knew what things she was thinking about, but
now wasn't the time for such a question.

Rafe and Dave carried two large steaming pizzas into the
dining room and set them on the table. Erik followed with
plates and forks and the salad.

They devoured the pizzas, then Doug reached for his cane.
"Thanks, everyone, for your part in this harrowing week. I'm
sorry Scott and Jake were shot."

"What's the latest update on them?" Erik asked.

"I was told by the doctor who treated me that Scott's wound
in his upper arm tore up his bicep. But he'll heal. He'll be

released tomorrow. Jake was hit in the side. He's still in intensive care after surgery."

"So we don't know the extent of Jake's injuries yet." Alison's eyes were downcast and her voice shook. "He tried to keep those guys from kidnapping me."

"Those were ruthless men." Rafe stacked plates and carried them to the kitchen.

Doug leveraged himself out of his chair, using his cane. "The food helped. I'm heading for the den to make a call to Hawaii. Let them know what happened."

"And I'll call Tricia. I'm sure she's enjoying herself, but I hope she'll be ready to fly home." Nick stood and grasped Doug's arm. "With that baby coming, I want her back here now. I'll call her from my car. Then I'm heading home for a very long night's sleep. But first I'm going to make sure you don't end up on the floor."

Doug grasped his cane, then took a step with his right foot. His knee buckled. Nick steadied him. Okay, he wasn't quite ready to walk on his own. How was he going to get upstairs to the bedroom later?

Once in the den, Doug sank onto the couch and pulled out his phone. "Thanks. I did need the help."

"And I'm glad you're finally admitting you're human." Nick smiled. An effort. They were all tired. "And now you rebuild. The agency. Your house. And you and Scott and Jake need time to heal."

"I'll buy another house and sell that lot. Great view out the back." He stretched out his right leg on the couch.

"You're already thinking ahead."

"Yeah." Wondering about Alison. Would today's events hurt or help his chances with her?

Nick stood by the door. "You and your agency can get back

to your normal business now. If that young woman with Armando calls again, have her call Chet or me."

"Armando is still out there. You mean our help is no longer needed?"

"Yeah, I guess that's what I mean. Go back to insurance fraud, finding lost children. The things you and your staff are very good at."

"And leave the cop work to the cops. The investigations."

"And the killing, if it comes to that."

"If Armando leaves us alone." He glared at Nick.

No smile this time from Nick. A return glare. "I'll be back tomorrow to check on you. Get some sleep." He left.

Doug made his call to Hawaii and talked to Kara, Dani, and his mother, and told them to stay as long as they wanted. That the cleanup was just beginning on this end. He was putting his phone away when Alison and Chet came into the den. Alison sat in a chair by the window. Too far away.

Chet sat on the other end of the couch. "The bureau has released a statement that the kidnap victims need time to recover and the investigation is ongoing. That Moreno was a drug lord and other members of his gang are still on the loose."

Alison's expression was guarded. Like she was shutting herself away again. He needed to talk to her. Too many people around.

"So, what happens next?" Doug eased back into the pillows at the end of the couch.

"There will be some formal hearings, with the DEA task force as part of the target." Chet's expression held pure disgust. "They hindered our investigation, and caused problems for everyone. If a tactical unit had gone in after Moreno as soon as the house was located, a lot of bloodshed would have been avoided. There would have been no abductions."

"Will the DEA cooperate while you work on the drug gang problems in Portland?" Alison asked. "Armando has a direct line to that cartel."

Will Siegel appeared at the den door. "And Armando has emptied the Harney house and they went separate directions in small groups."

"Did you follow anyone?" Chet asked.

"I tried but they knew I was on surveillance. They managed to ditch me." Will sat on a chair near the door.

"Do you have any useful information that will help us?"

"I have license plate numbers of most of the vehicles. I saw eight men and three women." Will took a folded sheet of paper from his pocket and handed it to Chet.

"Have you been to see Jake?" Alison asked. "How's he doing?"

"He had surgery to remove the bullet. No vital organs damaged, but the bullet had lodged against a rib. He's doing okay, but will stay in the hospital for now."

"How serious?" Doug asked. "Will he recover?"

"Eventually. Hensley had a talk with him. He plans to stay with the DEA, and keep his liaison position with the police here in town." Will smiled. "Hensley is sending him to the coast, to Waldport, to heal. Then he'll do surveillance on the coast for a while. To see if they can stop some drugs from getting to Armando."

"What about you?"

"I'd like to get a PI license and work for your agency. If you'll have me." He frowned. "I don't like how the DEA operates sometimes."

"Neither do I, and I do want you on the staff. I'm expanding and need good men and women." Doug shifted on the couch, stretching out his legs as best he could. "I'll get the building renovated. The agency up and running, as quickly as possible. We have cases on hold we need to tackle."

And Doug couldn't get comfortable and his head was still pounding, though he'd tried to ignore it. "I need to go upstairs and stretch out on a bed. I need sleep." And a chance to talk to Alison. Something he didn't want to voice out loud. Would she talk to him tonight? Or would she completely retreat into her shell?

"We get the hint," Chet said. "See you tomorrow. I'll have more information then." He left and Will followed.

"You could have asked them for help getting up the stairs." Alison's tone held a note of accusation.

He used the cane and levered himself off the couch. "I'll manage." He wasn't going to ask her for help.

"Dave. Rafe." Alison shouted out the door.

They appeared in the doorway. "Please help this stubborn, injured man up the stairs."

"Sure." Rafe grasped Doug's left arm and Dave took the right. Alison grabbed the cane out of his hand. Something flickered in her expressive blue eyes. An emotion. What did it mean?

CHAPTER 29

*a*lison followed the men up the stairs, then halted at the doorway to Doug's room. Rafe and Dave left Doug sitting on the side of the bed. Could she turn her back on Doug and go to her own room to sleep?

No, not yet.

"Thanks, guys." She tried to smile at them, but it wouldn't come. Not a happy emotion. Not tonight.

"You're welcome." Rafe gave her a salute and the men went down the stairs.

"Come here." Doug patted the bed at his side.

"You need to sleep. So do I." She stayed where she was though his eyes tugged at her, begged her.

"You have my cane."

She took it to him. He grabbed the cane with one hand and her arm with the other. And pulled her down at his side. "That's better. You were too far away."

He grasped her hand. To keep her there? Keep her from running?

Did she want to run away? Her thoughts and emotions were a jumbled mess. She didn't say anything, just stared into his dark eyes. Eyes smoldering with emotion. Was it desire?

"We need to talk." He tugged her closer.

"About what?" A stupid question, a product of her muddled mind.

"Six days of danger, chaos, death."

Not what she expected. "Okay."

"Two days ago you killed Kenny. Today I killed Moreno. They forced it on us. We had no choice. But we survived."

"It's a strange feeling, killing someone. Will it continue to haunt us, these deaths?"

"Not if we don't let it. We're alive. Still able to enjoy life."

He pulled her closer, against his body, and his arm went around her shoulders.

She tensed.

"Relax. I'm just offering you some comfort tonight."

She leaned into him, into his warmth, into his strength. It's what she needed right then.

"In my more lucid moments, while tied up on that floor, I promised myself one thing." He looked at her, those dark eyes flashing. "If I get out of this alive and you do too, I'm not wasting any more time hiding behind my disability, using my crippled legs as an excuse to keep to myself."

"Is that what you were doing?"

"I've been afraid to love again. Afraid I might lose someone else. And I have. Lindi."

A little flutter of hope cascaded through her. "What are you saying?"

"I'm not looking for any promises, no long-term commitment. If you're not ready for that yet." His words were quiet, sounding sincere. He was giving her time.

"I like my job. I don't want to jeopardize it."

"That's a relief. I was afraid you'd want to leave, after all the violence."

"No. I believe the agency will get back to a normal routine. That I can handle."

"Do you think these feelings we have for each other might not last?" His words sounded worried. Had she misjudged him?

"How can we know?"

"I know." He tightened his grip. Held her against his muscled chest. "What if I told you I've loved you for several years? Would that make a difference?"

"You have?" A huge shock wave reverberated through her. And that glimmer of hope brightened.

"Yes."

"We're a sad pair of loners." She pulled back so she could see his face.

"What do you mean?" A puzzled expression.

"I fell in love with you...maybe two years ago. I've tried to keep my feelings hidden."

"You certainly succeeded. Was that so you wouldn't jeopardize your job?" His eyes sparked.

"Yes. And the fact that there's a considerable difference in our ages. We were both hiding behind our roles. You as boss. Me as employee."

"Yes, we were. And I don't see a problem with the age difference. You're thirty-three and very mature. And I'm forty-eight now." He hesitated. "Unless you want children."

"No. I've never pictured myself as a mother. But our... session at the hotel showed me what was missing in my life." She held his gaze.

"Yeah. A rather spectacular eye-opener." He grinned, that electrifying smile of his lighting his face.

She felt the heat rise in her cheeks. Blushing at her age. "I'm willing to take a risk. I'm willing to follow my heart." A heart that was bursting with joy.

"And I'm willing to admit that I need somebody, that I don't have to stand alone. We have to trust that everything will come out right, for both of us."

"You have a daughter you need to get to know." She blurted it out, a little embarrassed.

"And I will. But Dani is going to live with my mother and keep her company and go to college here in Portland. They arranged it while in Hawaii."

"So, where do we go from here?"

"*Carpe diem.*"

"Seize the day?"

"Life is too short. We're going to live in the present, together. Then we can get to know each other better."

Is that what she wanted? Yes, as scary as it felt. "You don't have a house anymore. I have an apartment that needs cleaning up."

"We can use that apartment on the third floor for now, until we decide what to do next. Until we find a house, one we both want."

"You're not going to rebuild?"

"No. I don't want to live on that hillside anymore."

What a thing to be talking about. Buying a house. When she was sitting on the bed with a man she knew mostly as a boss. A man she'd made love with only once.

"You're thinking too much. We need to trust our feelings." He scooted closer. "I want to kiss you and then I want to crawl into bed and go to sleep by your side."

She leaned in and he pulled her into his arms and his lips met hers. Seeking, tasting, then devouring. The heat built between them. Her whole body was inflamed, engulfed with need. But he was injured.

He broke the contact and moved back. "My pounding head isn't ready for anything tonight. We need sleep."

"Yes. You're in pain. We're both sleep deprived. So we sleep tonight but we don't have to be in any hurry to get up in the morning." She said the words tentatively.

His smile was full of promises. "You're right. Tonight we sleep."

He pulled her to him for another kiss. "I do love you, very much."

"I love you too." Healing words. Trusting words. *Carpe diem*, indeed.

AUTHOR'S NOTE

Thank you for buying Dare to Conquer! I hope you enjoyed it. This book is number three in the Those Who Dare series. All the books in this extended series are connected to Landreth Investigations in Portland, Oregon. Book four, Dare to Hide, will be out in early 2019. Watch my website for more details.

http://barbararaerobinson.com

You can also subscribe to my newsletter on my website and receive advance notice of future publications in the series or future books.

ABOUT THE AUTHOR

Barbara Rae Robinson writes romantic suspense novels that sizzle with the heart-pounding rush of danger and the edgy emotions of falling in love. After her debut romance with Harlequin, Barbara turned her attention to combining romance with suspense. Her current project is an ongoing series of tales of death-defying heroic men and courageous women. Barbara lives in rural Oregon, close to Portland, the setting of her current series.

http://barbararaerobinson.com